"Spea... Lockett,"
TJ ... drawl.
"Whe... spent the
night in a bedroll?"

The seductiveness in his voice kicked at her imagination for what he might imply…until she assured herself he hadn't implied anything. Certainly nothing intimate. The question was a legitimate one.

"Not so long ago," Callie Mae said, her chin lifting from her own foolishness.

"So you'd best get down and we'll get ready to turn in," he said and dismounted with the grace of a man who'd done it all his life.

He strolled toward her and got her imagination going. That intimacy again. The inevitability that the two of them would be together.

Sleeping.

Side by side.

We'll get ready to turn in…

"Now?" she asked and hated herself for it.

"What's the matter, Callie Mae? Don't want to sleep with me?" he taunted.

* * *

Kidnapped by the Cowboy
Harlequin® Historical #901—June 2008

Author Note

In my last book, *Untamed Cowboy,* my readers met Carina Lockett and her daughter Callie Mae, who unwittingly became a pawn in a blackmail attempt led by Callie Mae's no-good father and overzealous grandmother. Readers met Penn McClure, too, who was determined to arrest a ring of counterfeiters master-minded by a man named Bill Brockway and save the Lockett legacy at the same time. They learned about the C Bar C ranch and the outfit devoted to the land, and how the cowboys would risk their lives right alongside Penn out of love for the cattlewoman and her daughter.

Kidnapped by the Cowboy continues the story. Ten years later, Callie Mae is a grown woman, and her legacy is threatened once again.

I've invented a son for Bill Brockway. After all these years, Kullen Brockway, alias Kullen Brosius, still has revenge festering in his blood against Penn and Carina, and he intends to use Callie Mae to finally satisfy it.

It's been great fun having the C Bar C cowboys in my head again. Especially TJ Grier, who is no longer the lanky wrangler he was then. He's all grown-up, and he has a love for Callie Mae to rival the ages.

I hope you enjoy their story.

PAM CROOKS

Kidnapped by the Cowboy

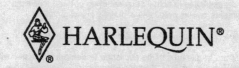
HARLEQUIN®

TORONTO • NEW YORK • LONDON
AMSTERDAM • PARIS • SYDNEY • HAMBURG
STOCKHOLM • ATHENS • TOKYO • MILAN • MADRID
PRAGUE • WARSAW • BUDAPEST • AUCKLAND

ISBN-13: 978-0-373-29501-2
ISBN-10:   0-373-29501-4

KIDNAPPED BY THE COWBOY

Copyright © 2008 by Pam Crooks

First North American Publication 2008

This edition published by arrangement with Harlequin Books S.A.

® and TM are trademarks of the publisher. Trademarks indicated with ® are registered in the United States Patent and Trademark Office, the Canadian Trade Marks Office and in other countries.

www.eHarlequin.com

Printed in U.S.A.

DON'T MISS THESE OTHER
NOVELS AVAILABLE NOW:

#899 THE LAST RAKE IN LONDON—Nicola Cornick

Dangerous Jack Kestrel was the most sinfully sensual rogue
she'd ever met, and the wicked glint in his eyes promised he'd
take care of satisfying Sally's *every* need....
Watch as the last rake in London meets his match!

#900 AN IMPETUOUS ABDUCTION—
Patricia Frances Rowell

Persephone had stumbled into danger and the only way to
protect her was to abduct her! But what would Leo's beautiful
prisoner do when he revealed his true identity?
Don't miss Patricia Frances Rowell's unique blend of passion
spiced with danger!

#902 INNOCENCE UNVEILED—Blythe Gifford

With her flaming red hair, Katrine knew no man would be
tempted by her. But Renard, a man of secrets,
intended to break through her defenses....
Innocence and passion are an intoxicating mix
in this emotional Medieval tale.

Prologue

❧❧❧

Amarillo, Texas, 1896

She'd learned to live in the shadows.

They became her refuge when her mind wouldn't rest. When the pain reared up like an angry demon to thrash at her insides and make her bleed. Set her heart to pounding and her body shaking and turning her fears hauntingly real.

Like now. Late at night.

The pain always came then. When it was dark and she was alone. Forcing her body to crave the whiskey that was slowly killing her.

But her soul needed comfort, her memories needed numbing.

Her mistakes forgiven, most of all.

Another swig of rotgut helped her breathe, and she leaned her head back against the rough siding of the horse barn. The scent of fresh-cut wood surrounded her and soaked into the fragile threads of her awareness.

The timbers were new. So new they had yet to feel the pelting from a summer rain or be dressed in their first coat of paint. They came together to form a structure the likes of which she'd never seen before, and the new barn, the grandest of gifts, would last a lifetime.

Like the C Bar C Ranch and its legacy.

Her gaze lifted to the house sprawled in the distance, perched like a giant beast on the hill. Every window had a light shining through it, and the night carried faint strains of laughter and music.

A party was being given by Carina Lockett McClure and her husband, Penn, to celebrate their daughter's return from a summer spent in Europe. Folks from all over the Texas Panhandle came to see Callie Mae and welcome her back home while flaunting their money, fancy clothes and high-society ways.

They wouldn't know about pain and shadows. They wouldn't need whiskey to help them survive.

She tried to feel contempt for them and failed. Her mistakes had always been her own.

She lifted the bottle again, but her tongue found only a trickle of liquor.

It didn't matter. She had more.

She was careful not to toss aside the empty container, evidence of her addiction. Instead, she tucked the bottle under her arm while using the other to brace herself against the side of the barn, her palm hardly aware of the roughness of the wood. Her gait was steadier this way. More sure. And she easily moved through the darkness toward the back door.

But suddenly, something didn't feel right.

She froze, her senses sluggish, her mind working to figure out why.

The sounds of music and laughter were barely discernible now. She swept an uneasy glance around her, but the silence, the moonlight, revealed nothing.

Only the scent of so much lumber seemed real.

She shook off her unease. She kept moving down the side of the barn, and rounding the corner, she halted again, this time her attention caught by tiny flickering lights in the distance. A couple dozen, at least. Torches spread out along a makeshift track.

The C Bar C outfit was indulging in some late-night horse racing. This far from the main house, distracted by their guests, Carina and Penn wouldn't see. If they did, they wouldn't approve. Racing, drinking and gambling were against the rules. The outfit would be doing all three.

Their secret was safe with her. She'd enjoyed the vices herself far too often in her younger days. Who was she to tell them it was wrong?

She shifted her attention to the door, unlocked as she'd known it would be. She fumbled with the latch. The new hinges squeaked from her pull, and the door swung open.

She slipped inside. The C Bar C horses hadn't been stabled yet, but lighting a lantern would be a surefire way of alerting someone she was up to no good, and even drunk, she wasn't that stupid. She knew where to go, the exact place where she'd hidden a brand-new bottle of Old Fitz.

She left the door partially open, needing what little moonlight that seeped inward to find her way. Gathering her courage, she veered left, toward a narrow corridor and a small apartment tucked behind the last stall. No light shone beneath the closed door. Cautious relief swept through her. She was foolish to be here, doing what she was doing. If anyone saw her, TJ especially…

Behind her, the hinges squeaked again.

She froze.

"TJ? Are you in here?"

Her heartbeat dipped at the young voice calling hesitantly into the darkness. The barn door opened wider. Moonlight spilled in. She pressed back against the wall, deeper into the shadows.

"Hey, TJ?"

Danny McClure, Penn and Carina's ten-year-old son, stepped inside, holding a lantern. He set the lamp down, then squatted, struck a match and lit the wick. Golden lamplight flared around him, and he straightened.

He was still dressed in his gray knee pants and coat, white shirt and tie. Which meant he'd come straight from his sister's party. All the way from the main house.

Alone.

To see TJ?

Her mind strove to figure it. TJ wouldn't have asked Danny to come. Not like this. Carina would never have allowed it, besides, nor would Penn, even to see one of the best wranglers in their outfit.

Which meant they didn't know Danny was here.

"I can take you to him."

She started at the unexpected male voice. Danny's dark head whipped toward the sound, a low drawl sliding smooth through the darkness. Footsteps approached. Out of the shadows, a man appeared. Short, wiry. In no hurry.

Unease crawled down her spine.

She knew all the ranch's cowboys, had cooked for them down at the bunkhouse one time or another. If she didn't know their names, she knew their faces.

And this one she'd never seen before.

At least, she didn't think so.

He wore his hat funny. Down over his face. On his nose, almost. Even in the dark.

Her heart began a slow, troubled thud...while her whiskey-numbed brain churned to place him.

To understand.

Danny cocked his head. "Who are you?"

The man halted. He smiled.

"A friend," he said.

"Of TJ's?"

His shoulder lifted in a careless shrug. "Something like that."

"Where is he?"

"I'm a friend of your father's, too," the man said. He smiled again.

She didn't like his evasiveness. Or the looks of that smile. She'd seen both too often from the men in her life. Men who never meant the things they said. Who only smiled like that when they wanted something.

Something wrong.

She swallowed and tried not to be afraid. For herself. For Danny. She didn't want to listen to what the nagging voice in her head tried to tell her.

"The lady said he'd be here." Danny took a sideways step, as if to check for himself the shadows behind the stranger.

The stranger took a step, too. So Danny couldn't.

"He's not," the man purred.

Danny's expression turned puzzled. "But she said he wanted to race with me down in the valley. She said the whole outfit was there, waiting."

It was what bound the two together like brothers, she knew. Their love for racing. Their sharing of the passion. The exhilaration and recklessness that fired their blood.

Danny shifted at the stranger's silence. One foot to the other. "Guess she was wrong, then, huh?"

He was trying to be brave, she realized, but apprehension threaded his words. She could feel his fear, building with her own. Higher with every pulsating second.

She didn't want him to feel the fear. To see how ugly life could be. Danny McClure was only a child, his world fiercely protected. Filled with love and happiness.

"I'll take you to him, Danny-boy. We'll find TJ together." The stranger reached toward him, slow and easy.

Her heart pounded harder.

The warning voice shouted louder.

Nobody called Danny McClure "Danny-boy." Ever. He despised the nickname. He always had, and every cowboy on the C Bar C—every single one—knew it, honored it and obeyed that one little rule.

Never call Danny "Danny-boy."

The stranger broke the rule. Because he didn't know. Because he wasn't C Bar C. And if she didn't do something to help Danny, if she didn't listen to that voice screaming inside her head, insisting there was no one else, no one else, no one else…

Oh, God. Oh, God.

She eased away from the wall, curled her fingers around the tall neck of the whiskey bottle tucked under her right arm.

"Come with me," the man said. "Let's find TJ, Danny-boy."

"No!" he shouted and leapt back, but the stranger was bigger, faster, and he grabbed Danny's arm with a curse.

The rage broke free. She burst from the shadows with a wild shriek. "Leave him alone!"

The stranger whirled toward her.

Danny's eyes widened in recognition, and if he said anything, if he called out her name, she didn't hear it, not when she was driven by the raging voice of fear inside her.

"Let him go. Let him go!" She hurtled toward them, her left arm lifting, her grip on the bottle desperate. The stranger twisted, shielding himself against her blow, but still she swung, hard, as hard as she could, and the glass crashed against his head. His hat flipped to the ground. He staggered back, and Danny broke free.

"Run, Danny!" she shouted.

The stranger bellowed, and he lunged for the boy, but Danny reacted, swinging the lantern to fend him off. The man's arm came up, deflecting the blow. The lantern sailed to the ground and shattered.

"Go, Danny!" she yelled, frantic, insistent, and she came at the stranger again, throwing herself at him with all the strength she had. He knew her now, knew that she was there and he pushed her off easily, as if she weighed nothing at all.

She catapulted to the ground with a jarring thud, but not before the jagged edges of the whiskey bottle still gripped in her fist slashed across his jaw. He blinked, momentarily stunned. The skin fell open, and a long line of crimson streamed down his face.

Flames exploded from the shattered lantern and licked along the floor toward the nearest stall, their fiery hunger frenzied, insatiable, for fresh lumber.

She stared, horrified.

Until a flurry of movement pierced the horror. Danny running for the door, and the stranger going after him, snarling his rage.

She scrambled to her feet and flung aside the piece of glass, her fear for Danny tearing through her. She had to save him, or he'd be taken from them all, and she stumbled down the narrow corridor, swathed in firelight, to the small apartment and the shotgun she knew was there.

TJ always kept the only weapon he owned propped in the corner, and she found it quickly, her fear building, giving her strength. The flames burned, blinding and fierce, yet somehow she managed her way through to the outside.

She ran until she found them, the shadowed shape of the stranger giving chase to the boy. She'd never learned to shoot, not really, and oh God, it was so dark. But she had to try.

For Danny, she had to make the stranger stop.

She halted, took aim, her eye fastened on the man's back. He turned then. A quick glance over his shoulder, for anyone in pursuit.

Seeing her, his step faltered.

She fired.

Time ceased to exist.

Her mind had lost its function, the ability to comprehend anything but the terrible mistake she'd made.

It was how TJ found her. Numb and mindless. On her knees in front of the unmoving shape. Guilty of one more wrong in her life.

TJ was the one thing she'd ever managed to get right, but he looked appalled at what she'd done. Stricken with grief.

Fear choked at her insides. She couldn't breathe, couldn't think. She knew only that she didn't deserve to live.

From somewhere on the fringes of her comprehension, horses' hooves thundered. Voices yelled. Flames roared into the sky.

Shadows hid her, but not for long. The darkness would never be her salvation again.

"Let me handle this," TJ said. He dragged in air, his voice unsteady but his words rough with urgency. "Don't say anything to anyone. Y'hear me? Don't say anything."

She whimpered and tried to understand, to know what he intended to do.

"Go," he said, giving her a hard nudge. "Get away from here."

Confusion swirled through her sluggish brain. "But—"

"*Go*, damn it."

The fear in her responded to his command, to the need for him to take care of her, like he'd always taken care of her.

And she fled into the night.

Chapter One

One Year Later

Callie Mae Lockett channeled her concentration on the men seated at the table with her. She could do this. She could fight three of the most powerful men in the Texas Panhandle.

Alone.

They had the Amarillo Hotel's lavishly appointed dining room to themselves. Dinner had been exquisite as always—roast sirloin of beef au jus and tender asparagus in cream sauce. The chocolate blanc mange had been heavenly, too. Now, only brandy glasses and crystal dishes holding ashes from expensive Reina Victorias remained on the starched white tablecloth—right alongside a detailed map of the sprawling C Bar C Ranch.

"This exposition will showcase the northern part of the state, Callie Mae." James T. Berry, a townsite developer, had been instrumental in growing Amarillo from a tent camp of railroad workers to the country's largest rural shipping point for cattle. "Folks will know we're more than cows and barbed wire out here."

"Oh?" She arched a brow and hid her annoyance with a cool smile. "I'm rather partial to those cows myself."

A fact every man at the table well knew. The C Bar C Ranch enjoyed a prominence in the area that cowmen with less range on their land deed envied. Thousands of head of cattle and more acres than most men could count made up the Lockett spread, all of it spearheaded by her mother.

Carina Lockett McClure. Her husband—Callie Mae's stepfather—Penn McClure, had been at her side every step of the way. Mother depended on him more than she'd admit, and over the past twelve years, they'd established the C Bar C as a formidable presence in the state of Texas.

One day, it'd all be Callie Mae's. Every square inch. The Lockett legacy.

Meeting with these entrepreneurs was the first real opportunity her mother had given her to hold the Lockett reins in her hands. To feel the breadth of her power in a world dominated by men.

To wield it.

How she handled herself would be ruminated and scrutinized by folks living in a four-state area. As if she was a prize steer on the auction block.

Callie Mae couldn't fail the test. She had to defeat their proposition to buy prime C Bar C land for ill-gained profit. She had to prove to her mother she could be as smart and ruthless as the best of them.

But mostly, she had to prove it to herself.

The fact the entrepreneurs wanted a piece of the section where the beautiful Tres Pinos Valley was located further sealed her resistance to the deal. She'd earmarked that land for herself to live on with her husband. To raise a family, now that she'd come of age to marry. She refused to be crowded out by a foolish exposition.

"Of course you're partial to those cows." Joseph Glidden, owner of one of the first cattle spreads in Texas, the Frying Pan Ranch, nodded in concession. "But folks need some place to go to be entertained 'round these parts. I'll guarantee the crowds will *flock* out here if we hold an exposition."

An event that would include horse racing and far too much drunken wagering. Contempt curled through Callie Mae. She knew the lure those things held for men, thanks to that no-good TJ Grier, once one of the C Bar C's best cowboys. Callie Mae and her mother stood together in refusing to allow racing and all the vices it brought with it to taint the C Bar C again.

"Can't you see how grand this venture will be?" Henry Sanborn owned enough property in the area to earn the title of Amarillo's founding father. He leaned forward, his eyes lit with excitement. "Hot-air balloons. Concerts. Exhibits. Cattle sales and contests. Fireworks!"

"What I *see*, Henry," she said firmly. "Is people's hard-earned money snatched up on races rigged to lose. I see harlots and con men taking advantage of the gullible. I see money wasted on whiskey and betting." She made a sound of disgust. "Need I say more?"

James puffed on his cigar. "Eighty acres, Callie Mae. That's all we're asking."

Her glance swiveled. "I'm sorry. No."

"The C Bar C won't *miss* the land. And we're willing to pay you top price to buy it."

"That's not the issue here, is it?"

"The issue is, the exposition could be a gold mine for everyone," Joseph said.

"The horse-racing part of it, you mean."

He hesitated. "The revenue would be a major factor, yes."

"Callie Mae." Henry's smile appeared forced. "It's clear the root of the problem here is your resistance to the sport the rest of us enjoy. Perhaps you should set aside your personal beliefs and think of this as a business matter, nothing more."

Callie Mae hung on tight to her poise. Mother would've been proud that she managed it.

"I believe men should work honestly for their money, Henry, and not have their fortunes handed to them by a racehorse," she said slowly. With enough emphasis that a child of three would understand. "Or have them taken away by one."

Amusement flickered across his features, but he had the sense to keep it banked. He inclined his head. "There are two sides to that coin, of course."

"And the business side of mine is to reject your offer to buy Lockett land."

Each man glanced at the other, and their demeanors turned grim. A tense silence descended over the table. Callie Mae waited for one of them to make the next move. She'd made hers and wouldn't budge.

"Perhaps it would be in our best interests to talk to your mother," Joseph Glidden said finally, finding fascination in the burning end of his cigar.

Callie Mae's nostrils flared. The insult stung. As a Lockett, she was capable of making this decision. She had the knowledge, the privilege. The power.

The threat to go around her and negotiate with her mother instead proved they saw Callie Mae not as an emerging cattle queen, heiress to the Lockett holdings, but as Carina Lockett McClure's daughter, and nothing more.

"It won't do any good," she sniffed.

"It might."

"We completely agree on the matter."

"Carina is a shrewd businesswoman. She'll see the advantages of our proposition."

Callie Mae gritted her teeth. "She's in California."

Callie Mae hadn't wanted them to know, hadn't wanted them to think of her as a mere substitute for her mother's absence. That she was their last resort, and an inexperienced one at that.

James's gray brow lifted. "Oh?"

"Penn felt she needed a change."

An uncomfortable moment passed.

"Of course," he said.

She steeled herself against the sympathy in his voice and refused to look at the pity in each of their faces. It'd been a year since her young brother had been killed, and there were days when she thought she'd accepted the loss and moved on with her life.

But there were other times, like now, when she knew she hadn't.

She stifled her hate for TJ Grier and pasted a smile on her mouth. "Mother has never seen the ocean, you know. Penn insisted on taking her there for—for a vacation. It took some doing, but he finally managed to get her on the train."

"It's good that he did. Carina works too hard. Harder, I suspect, since Danny died," James said, not unkindly.

"Yes."

She clasped her hands tightly in her lap. "Hard" failed to describe the way Mother had driven herself these past months, fighting the grief from TJ's betrayal and losing her only son. If Penn hadn't stepped in, the exhaustion would have destroyed her.

"Penn wants their whereabouts kept secret," Callie Mae added, lest the men attempt to contact them across the wires. "They won't be back for quite some time. The end of the month, at least." She drew in a breath, forced herself to stop babbling over the information she'd wanted to keep private. "So you see, gentlemen, you must deal with me. There's no one else."

"We're prepared to draw up a charter of incorporation tonight." Henry tapped the sheaf of papers in front of him. "What'll it take to convince you to let us get started?"

At the desperation in his expression, a sense of control returned to Callie Mae. "I do believe you've tried everything already."

"But we're not giving up." Resolve threaded his words. "There's not a better place in the Texas Panhandle to hold that exposition. We need that land to make it happen."

"My answer stands. Now, shall we call it an evening, gentlemen?" She stood and shook each man's hand as they rose with her. "Until we meet again."

"And we will." Henry gathered his papers and tucked them under his arm. "You have my word on it."

"You'll find nothing has changed."

He grunted, muttered something under his breath, and they left. After the door closed behind them, silence filled the dining room.

Callie Mae let out a slow breath. Eased back down into her chair. And turned to the man beside her.

Kullen Brosius looked unexpectedly troubled sitting there with his fingers steepled and his ankle crossed over his knee. Dressed in a high-priced gray suit and white shirt, he looked impossibly handsome, too.

Up until the day she died, he'd been her grandmother, Mavis Webb's, attorney and had drawn up her most important papers, including the inheritance Callie Mae stood to gain upon her twenty-third birthday, coming in a few weeks' time. Her grandmother had trusted him implicitly, and so did Callie Mae.

"You could've said something, you know," she said, fighting a pout. "Maybe then, they wouldn't have been so persistent."

Kullen sat up straighter. Sighed heavily. And leveled her with his hazel gaze. "The land isn't yours to sell, Callie Mae. I chose to keep from revealing that particular piece of information for obvious reasons."

She searched his expression for signs of teasing. And found none. But two could play his game. Her mouth curved in amusement. "Well, if those acres aren't mine, my dear Kullen, then whose are they?"

"TJ Grier's."

Her amusement died. "That's not funny."

"It's true. Richard informed me of the matter only recently." His mouth quirked. "And Richard never makes mistakes."

Richard Randolph was her mother's lawyer. He'd handled her affairs since the time she and Penn had married. His revered position in the Lockett dynasty was one Kullen hoped to have for himself one day. Why hadn't Richard told her of Mother's plan?

Kullen slid the big map across the tablecloth and positioned it in front of her. He tapped his finger on the very spot Henry Sanborn had outlined in bold black as the perfect location for the exposition. "Carina earmarked this section of land for TJ last year as a gift. A bonus, if you will, for being her favorite cowboy." Kullen's lip curled. "I had no idea Henry and the others chose it for the event until this meeting."

The part about TJ being Mother's favorite was true,

she knew. He always had been, for as long as Callie Mae could recall.

But still she resisted.

"No," she said. "There must be some mistake. She would've told me. Of *course*, she would've told me."

"You were in Europe at the time, traveling with Mavis. You were gone the whole summer. Perhaps it slipped her mind."

It wasn't like Mother to be so careless. And yet, soon after Callie Mae's return, Danny had been killed. Their lives were filled with chaos and heartache.

"It doesn't matter why she never told you, anyway." He regarded her with the shrewdness that made him the fine attorney he was. "What *matters* is what you're going to do about those eighty acres."

Callie Mae stilled. He was right, of course. Because suddenly, everything had changed. She wasn't in control anymore.

TJ Grier was.

Once Henry Sanborn and the others found out TJ owned those prime acres laying smack dab in the middle of the C Bar C, they'd find him and make him the same generous offer they'd made Callie Mae.

Maybe more.

And he'd take it, given his greed and disgusting penchant for horse racing. How much more convenient could the exposition be?

Kullen sat a moment, watching her, and she sensed how his thoughts mirrored hers. No wonder he looked so grim.

She thought of Danny, of the beautiful Tres Pinos Valley. "I can't let him do it."

"No," Kullen said.

"I have to find him. Insist that he not—"

She halted and fought the first stirrings of panic and frustration. Could she do it? Would he even listen?

It'd been so long since she'd seen TJ, had *wanted* to see him, that—

"I know where he is," Kullen said. "We can ride out today. Now, in fact."

The C Bar C was just about the only home TJ had ever had. Thinking of him living somewhere different was vaguely unsettling—until she stopped herself from thinking it. TJ lost his esteemed place in the C Bar C outfit through his own fault. No one else's.

Yet her belly lurched at the prospect of seeing him again. The last time had been awful. The night Danny had died. She could still feel the pain, the despair, from what TJ had done.

But she had to go to him. To keep horse racing and its demoralizing grip away from the C Bar C for as long as she could. To keep the beauty of Tres Pinos Valley for herself.

Her resolve strengthened. "I'll meet with him and inform him I won't tolerate racing, gambling and drunkenness on the C Bar C under any circumstances. I'll *insist* he not sell that land to Henry and the others."

Kullen smiled, as if he looked forward to the challenge she'd taken on.

"You're a Lockett, you know," he murmured. "You have the power."

The faint scent of brandy lingered in the air between them. His words soothed her, strengthened her, reminded her of the legacy she was bound to uphold, and her misgivings faded.

He lowered his head and touched his lips to hers. She sensed an odd reservation about him, as if he remained troubled, and she eased closer to assure him. To assure herself. But before she could deepen the kiss, he pulled away.

"Shall we?" he asked.

He stood and extended his hand. Skirts rustling, she stood, too, and twined her fingers through his.

Seeing his smooth skin and perfectly-trimmed nails reminded her that Kullen Brosius had never roped a calf in his life. Had never strung barbed wire, had never sucked in dust on a cattle drive.

He was the farthest thing from a cowboy she'd ever had the pleasure to meet.

And she was going to marry him. As her husband and shrewd-thinking attorney, he'd bring a new dimension to the C Bar C. A modern one. A piece of big-city charm and intelligence to the Lockett legacy.

But she hoped he had the guts to fight the likes of TJ Grier.

Chapter Two

"You've got yourself a winner in him, TJ," Boomer Preston said, both elbows braced on the fence rail. "I can feel it."

Keeping his thumb steady on the stopwatch, TJ Grier's gaze stayed glued to the black, sleek-coated stallion thundering around the track. He didn't want to agree with his old friend, who had more horse sense than anyone in the entire state of Texas. He didn't want to feel as if Blue Whistler would be his salvation from twelve months of pure hell.

But he did.

Most likely, he'd only jinx himself for it, but after the rotten turn his life had taken last year…well, a man needed hope that things would get better.

Blue Whistler was his hope, all right. In spades.

"Here he comes." Boomer's loud voice, which had earned him his nickname, rose even louder in anticipation.

TJ tensed, his thumb ready—the thoroughbred streaked past, throwing back clods of dirt—and the stop button instantly clocked the finish time. One look at the watch's dials, and Boomer let out a whoop of delight.

"Hot-damn! He just keeps getting better, don't he?" Boomer declared, his grin wide beneath his thick, almost-white moustache.

TJ stared at the clock. "He's two point seven seconds faster than he was yesterday when he ran the mile. *Damn*."

"Damned *fine* is what he is, TJ. Woo-wee!"

The jockey, Lodi Baldwin, slowed the stallion, eased him into a turn and trotted back toward them.

"How'd he do?" he called out.

TJ quoted the time, and a triumphant grin split the young man's face. He reined in at the fence, his knees pulled up from the high stirrups.

"Blue's ready, TJ," he said. "He's feeling good. He wants to race."

"Seems so, doesn't it?"

TJ's reverent gaze soaked in the sight of his prized thoroughbred. Even sweat-slick and dirty from the track, he was a beauty. Thickly muscled, with long, strong legs. Deep-chested. He had a proud streak in him, too. A touch of wildness, evident in the arrogant way he held his head. As if he knew the speed he was capable of and he defied anyone to doubt him.

"He's going to win in Fort Worth," Lodi said, still grinning. "Don't you think, Boomer?"

"He's got a good chance, Lodi. Real good."

TJ's gut clenched. They'd been training for the race in Fort Worth for weeks. The competition, held in conjunction with a prestigious stock show, would be Blue's first. TJ's, too, as his owner. Everything TJ could beg, steal or borrow was tied up in this horse. If something went wrong, if Blue put in a poor showing, TJ would be bitterly disappointed.

Devastated, even more.

But the need to win wasn't just for the money. It went deeper. An into-his-soul kind of deep.

He pushed Fort Worth from his mind. Forced himself to concentrate on the mundane. Chores that needed to be done. A horse who needed care. The best of it, from all of them.

"That's it for today. Let's get him hosed down, Lodi," TJ said, straightening from the fence. "I'll make sure his stall is ready."

"Sure thing, TJ." The jockey gathered up the reins, but on an afterthought, he halted. "Hey, maybe next time, we won't have to go as far as Fort Worth to race. There's talk about hosting a big exposition right here."

TJ stilled. "Yeah?"

"Somewhere on the C Bar C. Supposed to have a racetrack and everything."

Jesus. A racetrack. On the C Bar C.

"But the McClures are fighting it. The daughter, especially. What's her name?" Thinking on it, Lodi rubbed his chin.

A moment passed. TJ braced himself to say the words.

"Callie Mae." His voice rumbled. "Her name is Callie Mae Lockett."

"That's it."

Like a kicking, angry filly, her image reared up out of the past and into TJ's mind, until he roped it back and pushed her image into submission.

"Guess she's meeting with some of the local big-wigs to hash it all out," Lodi continued.

TJ kept his features impassive, his mind blank. He had all he could do to stand there and follow the jockey's conversation.

"We'll see what happens." Lodi shrugged. "But an event like that? Why, folks would come from miles around to see the horses run. The prize purses would be a fortune." Blue snuffled, and Lodi absently patted the sleek neck. "Sure would make this part of the Panhandle look good. If the Lockett woman had any sense, she'd jump at the chance to have the exposition on her land. Hell, her spread is so big, she won't even notice it's there."

Boomer grunted, his opinion of its size—and the woman who owned it—obvious. "You wouldn't think so, would you?"

TJ refused to look at him. Boomer knew as well as he did that Callie Mae would never agree. Never. Not after what happened...

"None of our business what she'll do," he said roughly. "Blue Whistler *is* our business, though, and he needs cooling down, like I said."

"Sure." Lodi hurriedly took up the reins again. "I'll get right on it, TJ."

"I'll go with him," Boomer said. "Have to make sure the rest of the work is getting done, too."

TJ knew he spoke of the new groomer they'd hired. Emmett Ralston had been slow to learn his job and required some extra supervising. TJ gave a curt nod of thanks and wished he could shake off the past as easily as Boomer did.

"You going to make it back in time for supper?" TJ asked.

"Tell Maggie I'll be there." Boomer ducked under the rails to follow Lodi, but he halted at the sight of a carriage rumbling down the lane. He sighed. "Looks like we got callers. I'll go see to 'em first."

Callers.

His mood worsening, TJ turned his back on them, slid the stopwatch into his shirt pocket and headed toward the stables. Whoever it was wouldn't be coming to see him. Not since he'd gotten out of prison had anyone *ever* come to see him.

And that's how he wanted it.

Most of the time.

He swore and blamed Lodi for bringing it all back. The decision and mistakes he'd made a year ago that destroyed everything he'd ever worked for. His hopes. Dreams. His pride and good name. How all he'd done had cost him his home on the C Bar C and every friend he'd known there.

Including the woman who'd been determined to see him hang.

Callie Mae Lockett.

Once, his need for her ran hot through his blood.

Not anymore.

Yet hearing her name, saying it—

Suddenly, inevitably, the raw burn of the past flared high and seared deep, as crippling as it'd been then. The weight of the memories, their ugliness, staggered him. Taunted him with all he'd lost.

He bent, grasped his knees and sucked in air. Waited for the burn to pass. The burn that was always there inside him, never going away…

A young life lost.

But another's saved.

God, it was so unfair.

The burn flowed, ebbed, faded. TJ drew in another breath. He straightened. And breathed again.

Life went on.

He'd survived.

Everyone survived.

Except Danny McClure.

"TJ? Are you all right?"

Maggie's voice pierced the turmoil spiraling through him. For her, more than anyone, he had to be strong. Unaffected. She was all he had. They had only each other.

Mother and son.

He turned toward her. Levi's and a baggy cotton shirt covered her wiry frame. She strode toward him looking boyish and tough, but TJ knew how fragile she was. If he didn't take care of her, she'd break, like aged porcelain.

"I'm fine." Hoping to prove it, he managed a smile.

She halted, her head tilted back to study him. The breeze plucked at her hair, gray and mostly ignored except for the single braid she always wore. Years of whiskey, men and heartache had branded themselves into her skin, aging her a decade more than she owned.

Her worried gaze delved into his until the creases in her face softened. She touched his cheek with a gentle hand, as if to soothe the pain she suspected still simmered within. "I heard Boomer yelling. I gather Blue had a good run this afternoon?"

"His best so far." TJ draped his arm around her shoulders and thought again how small she was. How much she needed him, would probably always need him. Her arm slid around his waist. Together, they headed toward the stables. "Boomer thinks he'll win."

"Oh, TJ. I'm almost afraid to hope."

He pulled open the door, and the rickety hinges wobbled. He made a mental vow to replace every damn hinge on the place, and a whole lot more besides, if Blue brought home the winner's purse.

He ushered his mother through. "Reckon it's hope that got us this far, Maggie. Don't be afraid of it."

She stepped away while he tugged the door closed, jiggling the handle to make sure it latched. When he turned back to her, tears shimmered in her eyes.

"There's not a man more deserving than you to win

that race, TJ Grier. I've been prayin' every night for it to happen."

The vulnerability in her expression and the quaver in her voice moved him. He refused to show it, lest he upset her more. His mouth crooked. "Most likely every man with a horse in that race is doing the same thing. Praying every night to win."

"Doesn't mean they deserve it like you do."

TJ didn't know if he deserved much of anything. He just knew he wanted the victory. Wanted it so much, it was downright pathetic.

The sound of Boomer's jovial voice seeped into the stable, and TJ's glance lifted to the nearest window. The visitors' carriage had turned off the lane and pulled up in the drive. An expensive rig, from the looks of it. A late-model runabout, leather top gleaming in the late afternoon sun. Boomer strode over to greet them.

Somewhere down the line of stalls, one of the broodmares whickered, reminding TJ why he was in here. To see to the readiness of Blue's stall. He pulled his gaze from the couple sitting in the buggy's seat and banked his curiosity about why they'd come, angling his body away from the window to shut them out.

He'd never considered himself an envious man, but their obvious wealth only served to remind him of his own poor state of affairs—and that he'd gotten damned weary of them.

He contemplated his mother, who owned nothing except the responsibility for her sins. She deserved more. Happiness. Fun. Some long overdue female pampering.

"Come to Fort Worth with us, Maggie," he urged. Again.

As always, the prospect seemed to terrify her. "Me? Rub elbows with all those hoity-toity folks?"

"I'd like you to see Blue run."

"I don't even own a decent dress."

"I'll buy you one. Fort Worth's a big town. Lots of stores there."

"Oh, TJ." She sighed, the sound vaguely wistful. Scared, more. "You don't understand."

"Yes, I do."

Her gaze turned troubled. "I'm nothing like them. I wouldn't fit. And the last thing I want to do is embarrass you."

"Embarrass me?"

"They'd just turn their noses up at ol' Maggie Grier."

He steeled himself against the way she saw herself. Unworthy. "We'd be there with you—Boomer and me. Lodi, too. You wouldn't have to face anyone alone."

"Folks like her, out there," Maggie said, staring over his shoulder as if he'd never spoken. "They'd be everywhere at the racetrack."

TJ couldn't help himself. He turned. The couple had climbed down from the runabout and strode toward the corral. Toward Blue. Boomer met them coming, talking and gesturing in his loud voice.

"Look at her, TJ," Maggie said, her words barely above a whisper. "You can just about smell her money from here. That dress of hers—how much do you suppose it cost?"

Through the glass pane, his gaze clung to the woman. She kept her hand tucked in her companion's arm, and the wide-brimmed contraption she wore on her head prevented TJ from getting a good look at her face.

But there was something about her. The alluring sway to her hips...

The fine hairs stood up on the back of his neck. He leaned closer to the glass, swiped at a fine layer of dirt to see through it better—and stared harder.

The air of confidence she carried about her. The control. That blood-warming package of femininity, fashion and grace.

He swore. Told himself it wasn't possible, that it was only a figment of his imagination stirred up by Lodi's announcement of an intended exposition on the C Bar C. Teeth gritted, TJ's glance swung to the man with her, but they'd moved beyond his range of view.

He swore again and bolted away from the window. He sprinted past the line of stalls, past the tack room and toward the door at the back of the stables.

"TJ." Maggie sounded alarmed as she hurried after him. "What is it?"

He ignored her, yanked open the door and burst outside. The corral was closer here. In plain view. Emmett was inside the rails and appeared oblivious to their visitors while he fiddled with attaching the end of a hose to the water pump. Lodi walked toward them with Blue on a lead rope, already stripped of his racing saddle.

The door clattered shut behind TJ. Boomer swung around at the sound. Whatever he'd been saying died on his lips, but the grim set to his mouth declared he'd been feeling less than friendly with his visitors.

In unison, the man and woman turned, too.

Recognition slammed into TJ. It'd been a long, hate-filled year since he'd breathed the same air as Kullen Brosius, the man who conspired to put him through a farce of a trial and long months of jail time. Seeing him now, with Callie Mae, set the hate on fire.

Maggie grasped his arm, as if she wanted to spare him from the burning. "Let's go back inside, son."

He shrugged free. Strode forward with a purpose that gave his dreams of revenge life. He would've rammed his fist down Kullen's shyster-lawyer throat if Boomer hadn't stepped in front of him and prevented it.

"Easy, TJ," he hissed. "You want to end up back in jail?"

TJ shoved him back; Boomer caught himself with a quick step. Yet despite the fury raging through him, TJ stayed put. Boomer was right. He'd be a fool to destroy the life he'd worked hard to put back together, just for the pleasure of breaking the man's damn neck.

"Well, well, well," Kullen drawled, looking pretty in his shiny leather shoes and fancy Hereford suit. "We meet again, don't we?"

"You son of a bitch," he growled.

"Let it go, TJ." Boomer barked the warning. "You don't have to talk to either of 'em."

This time, TJ refused to listen. He intended to talk, all right. Seeing Callie Mae now hadn't been in his plans. It was too soon. He wasn't ready.

But she was here, and so was Kullen, and if it was the last thing TJ ever did, he intended to find out exactly what happened the night Danny died.

Chapter Three

If Callie Mae hadn't been so determined to keep TJ from his vices and to save Tres Pinos for herself, she would've made sure she never laid eyes on him ever again, but there he was. In the flesh. Tall, rugged, disgustingly handsome—and looking mad enough to bite a rattlesnake.

Unexpectedly, her heart jumped to her throat. She blamed it on the quick rush of hate she'd kept festering inside her for so long. Told herself her reaction to seeing him again after all these months had nothing to do with him being one of her mother's best cowboys. Or that he had the maddening ability to turn the heart of most every female in the entire Texas Panhandle with his damned charm and virility.

No. Her reaction had everything to do with his betrayal—her anger at the actions that cost her young brother his life.

She stiffened, dragged her eyes off him and met

Maggie Grier's gaze instead. The woman suffered great shame from the crime her son had committed; the pain from it still showed on her face. Yet Callie Mae read the worry there, too. The apprehension. What did she think Callie Mae would do? Shoot TJ where he stood?

Unexpectedly, her heart dipped. God knew the man deserved it, but she wouldn't stoop so low. She had her pride, after all. She just had to fight to hang on to it.

She recalled her purpose in coming to see him. To keep the exposition with its insufferable horse racing and the vices that came with it off his eighty acres. Her success in convincing him would require every bit of her tolerance, wits and determination, and she gathered her courage to face him.

"Hello, TJ." She managed to keep her tone cool, aloof. In control.

His eyes, dark as saddle leather, swung from Kullen and slammed into her. Their ferocity rocked her with the warning that she'd underestimated the fury simmering inside him.

"Whatever you're up to with him, Callie Mae, you can damn well forget it," he snapped.

Her courage slipped. She yanked it back up again. "I've a matter to discuss with you, that's all."

"I'll bet you do."

She ignored his sarcasm. "It won't take long." She lifted her chin and speared him with her most haughty glare. "But before I begin, I insist you behave in an upright and civil manner to both of us so that we may proceed accordingly."

"You want civil, darlin'? You want upright?" His voice, low and lethal, slid shivers up her spine. "Funny. Last time we met, both of you were inclined to be neither."

She flinched. The last time...God, the pain and grief from losing Danny had been unbearable. The need to make TJ pay for his actions, consuming.

She bore through the memories and refused to feel guilt. Or let him sway her from what she had to do. "I need to talk to you. About your ownership of Tres Pinos Valley, that is."

She hated the thread of desperation in her voice. If the man had a shred of curiosity about her purpose, his animosity did a fine job of hiding it. Yet, something akin to surprise flickered across his dark expression before he quickly banked it.

"Yeah? Well, I have a thing or two to say to you, too," he said.

"Now's not the time, TJ," said Boomer.

TJ shifted toward the older man, his jaw hardening. "Too much time has passed."

"Maybe. But you'd be a fool to talk now before you're ready. And you know you're not." He shot a cold look toward Kullen. "Best climb back into your rig and ride out, y'hear? Take Miss Lockett with you."

Callie Mae stiffened. His rudeness stung. She'd never met the man before, but most every rancher in the Panhandle knew of his expertise in horseflesh. Burly-chested, with thick white sideburns and moustache, he clearly had a strong and loyal friendship with

TJ, too. The way Boomer kept his meaty fists clenched, as if he was ready to fight for TJ, well, it was obvious he had no intention of letting TJ talk to her.

Not that TJ seemed so inclined.

Worse, Callie Mae had the disadvantage. She didn't know what TJ was or wasn't ready for, but Boomer was determined to protect him, and his mother kept staring at her, looking terrified.

Callie Mae's determination wavered.

She needed to regroup, change her tactics. She had to find a way to talk to TJ alone and give herself the advantage.

"Go on." Boomer made a shooing motion, as if she was a pesky critter to be chased away.

She squared her shoulders and hung on to her pride. *Lockett* pride. If anyone here expected her to beg TJ for his attention, then they'd be sorely disappointed.

"Let's go, Kullen," she said.

She pivoted, flaring her skirt hems, but Kullen grasped her elbow with unexpected firmness, stopping her. Her startled glance flew upward.

She encountered his smile. A shrewd curving of his lips that showed his amusement from being in control. That he enjoyed its power. But mostly, his smile hinted of secrets—a few choice aces tucked inside his sleeve, waiting for him when he needed them most.

"Certainly." He pulled her closer, a possessiveness he didn't often show. Until now. He cocked his head toward TJ. "Do tell. What have you been doing since they sprung you out of jail?"

TJ's expression darkened. "None of your damned business."

Kullen appeared unaffected by the man's gathering wrath. He swept an arm outward, indicating their surroundings. "Living on this horse farm. Working with horses all day, every day. Guess it'd get you to thinking about racing them again, wouldn't it? Wait." He halted. Feigned surprise. "Is that a thoroughbred racehorse behind you? Well, I'll be damned. It is."

Callie Mae froze. Her mind veered past Kullen's mockery to lock on one word and its implication.

Racehorse.

TJ breathed a curse. His glance shot toward Boomer.

Boomer's glance shot toward TJ.

And Callie Mae's lifted to the regal stallion behind them, held on a lead rope by a youth, barely into his twenties, small-boned and shaggy-haired.

A jockey.

"I believe his name is 'Blue Whistler,' my lovely Callie Mae." Kullen's smile deepened, as if he reveled in the advantage he held. The knowledge that no one knew he possessed until now. "But they call him Blue."

"Oh, God." Maggie sounded alarmed. "How does he know so much about us?"

"I know you're heading to Fort Worth soon, too," Kullen said smoothly. "That beautiful horse is all signed up to race at the stock show there."

"Please." Maggie took a pleading step forward.

TJ flung an arm out, holding her back. "Stay out of it, Maggie."

"Just leave him alone, Mr. Brosius, will you?" she persisted. "Leave him alone."

"Boomer. Take her into the house," TJ ordered.

But Boomer didn't move. "I'm not leavin' just yet."

"How could you, TJ?" Callie Mae demanded with an appalled quiver in her voice.

His gaze slammed into hers; his eyes glittered hard and cold. "You were always quick to think the worst of me, Callie Mae."

"Didn't Danny's death mean anything to you? Was it so easy to forget how he died?" Her composure cracked. Furious hurt burst out and flowed free. "How can you not think of what your disgusting penchant for racing and its vices cost me and my family?"

"There's not a day that goes by when I don't think of it." His fists clenched, as if it was all he could do to keep from grabbing her. "It cost me plenty, too, Callie Mae." The words rumbled from him. "Damn you for thinking it hadn't."

Her lip curled. She'd been damned by him, all right. For the rest of her life. "What did it cost you? A few months in jail? A little tarnish to your reputation?"

"More than that." He fairly shook from the avowal. "*More.*"

A sudden rush of tears stung her eyes, and she blinked them away. Seeing him brought everything back and left her hurting and vulnerable all over again.

She'd made a foolish mistake coming out here.

She'd allowed her pride to slip, and now, *now* she'd made a spectacle of herself in front of him. And his mother. Kullen and Boomer Preston and—

She halted her pitying thoughts and drew herself up. "I don't believe you. Do you hear me, TJ?" she asked. "I don't believe you."

A chilling calm came over him. "Too bad you don't, Callie Mae, because it's not over yet. You're going to realize that, if it's the last thing I do."

"Oh, it's over, TJ." Kullen's handsome mouth twisted in a smirk. "Because you'll always be a child-murderer, won't you? Nothing will ever change that."

For a moment, no one spoke, no one moved, from the harsh reminder of the price TJ would forever pay.

Only Kullen seemed unaffected. "You'll never work for the C Bar C again. In fact, you'll never work for anyone around here. You're ruined as a cowboy."

The words swarmed through Callie Mae like a plague, leaving her stomach churning and her head dizzy but her mind clinging to the mantra she'd needed to survive the grief.

He deserved it, he deserved it, he deserved it.

No matter what she thought, he didn't deserve it.

TJ steeled himself against the look on Callie Mae's face. She didn't know how everything had gone horribly wrong that night. No one did. But the decision he'd made had plummeted his life into a hell he couldn't have imagined.

But it was going to get better. Once he had his revenge.

With Blue Whistler's help.

"What's the matter, TJ?" Kullen taunted. "Don't have anything to say for yourself?"

His vengeful thoughts reshaped to focus on the man in front of him. "You've said it all, haven't you?"

TJ gritted his teeth to keep from saying more. He'd learned the hard way there were times when a man had to fight to defend himself. Other times, like now, when he shouldn't.

"Get me away from him, Kullen." Chin quivering, Callie Mae spun toward her carriage.

TJ wasn't sure what got to him first—the tears she tried so hard to keep from spilling, or that she hated him so much that she couldn't bear to be within spitting distance of him.

Neither mattered except that there was so damned much he needed to say to her.

"Callie Mae, wait!" he said.

He took a long stride toward her, but Kullen moved right in front of him. Stopping him.

"You don't think she'll let you lay your murdering hands on her, do you?" he purred.

Every muscle in TJ's body quivered with the need to shut the man's mouth up for good. "Go to hell."

"I'd rather see *you* burn there first," Kullen said, amused.

"You'd best get out of here, Kullen." Boomer's voice bellowed. "Or you'll be fighting two of us."

"Oh, God. Please, no trouble," Maggie begged, looking frantic. "Just leave with her, will you?"

Callie Mae's glance jumped from one to the other. "Take me home, Kullen. Now."

TJ planted a hand on the man's shoulder to thrust him aside. He couldn't let her leave until she'd heard him out. "He conspired against Danny, Callie Mae. He's responsible for everything that happened that night."

She sucked in an appalled breath, and her mouth opened, but if she said something, the sudden fist into his gut kept him from hearing.

Pain exploded. TJ doubled over; the force of Kullen's hit sent him sprawling backward. His body rammed into Lodi, still holding Blue on his lead rope. Both of them slammed into the horse's belly.

Maggie screamed. Boomer yelled.

Blue whinnied in alarm. He reared, flailing his long legs, and instant fear shot through TJ.

The stallion had to be kept calm. An injury to those valuable legs this close to the Fort Worth race would be devastating. And the wild look in his eyes, as if he sensed impending violence, was terrified by it...

"Lodi, get him out of here."

At TJ's terse command, the jockey grappled for the lead rope. "Right away, TJ."

"Not so fast," Kullen said.

A hammer clicked.

Lodi froze.

Slowly, TJ turned, his instincts warning that things had just gone from bad to worse.

"Kullen. What are you *doing?*" Callie Mae demanded.

"Put that damn gun down," Boomer bellowed.

The afternoon sun glinted on the brass frame of a Colt derringer Kullen leveled at TJ's chest. "He'll listen to you now, Callie Mae. Go ahead. Tell him you want your land back."

TJ didn't care about any land, hers or anyone else's. He only knew she had to believe him before it was too late.

And time was ticking.

"He's not the man you think he is, Callie Mae," TJ said, hearing the desperation in his own voice. "For Danny's sake, you have to trust me."

"Kullen, what does he mean?" she demanded.

Kullen ignored her. He waved the derringer at Lodi. "Lodi, hand Blue's rope over to Emmett."

No one noticed the groomer had left the corral and stood nearby, watching, waiting.

No one except Kullen.

Lodi jerked back at the command. "Why?"

"Because I told you so."

Lodi shot a confused glance at TJ.

Who shot a glance at Boomer.

Who shot him a glance back that said "I'll take care of it."

TJ's muscles coiled, one by one. "Give Emmett the rope, Lodi."

Blue nickered, low in his throat, as if he could smell the tension in the air.

"If you're sure, TJ," Lodi said, still hesitant.

"I am."

Emmett stepped closer and snatched the rope from

the jockey—Boomer made his move and pushed the groomer roughly aside.

But before Boomer could grab hold of the hemp, a shot cracked through the air. He grunted and spun. Blood spurted onto his jacket sleeve, and he toppled to the ground with a thud.

TJ roared and lunged for the rope himself, but Emmett moved a heartbeat faster and slapped a heavy hand against Blue's flank.

The stallion reared with a terrified, ear-shattering shriek. TJ had all he could do to evade those powerful, flailing legs, and grab for the rope at the same time.

He missed.

"Hee-yah! Hee-yah!" Emmett yelled.

Before TJ could even *think* it could happen, Blue bolted, mind-numbingly fast.

Time stood still.

But the stallion kept moving, running with the speed that made him so spectacular, and in that one, horrible moment, TJ knew he'd lost everything.

If he didn't get Blue back again.

Enraged, he whirled toward Kullen. "You scheming son of a bitch!"

Kullen lifted the derringer and aimed the barrel at TJ's chest, but TJ hurtled toward him like a brainless locomotive, uncaring if he was shot or killed, because without Blue, he had nothing. Nothing. The hammer fell back—and Callie Mae screamed.

"No-o, Kullen!"

She threw herself against him, and the derringer

flew from his grip. TJ dove and scooped up the weapon, then rolled to his back with his finger sure on the trigger—all in one snarling motion.

Kullen scrambled for footing; suddenly, a switchblade appeared in his hand, and he came at TJ with the blade held high. But no matter how sweet putting a bullet into the bastard's heart would be, death was too good for him.

He was entitled to some suffering, too.

Deliberately, TJ lowered the barrel. And fired. The bullet found Kullen's thigh and shattered bone. The knife dropped, and he went down screaming.

"Oh, my God!" Her face colorless, Callie Mae stood riveted, her eyes wide on the bloodied leg.

TJ leapt to his feet and stepped toward her, hooking his arm roughly around her shoulders.

"You're coming with me," he growled, pressing the derringer to her temple. She had to know he meant business. That she had to come with him. To make her believe. She had to know the truth.

"Lodi. Don't just stand there with your jaw hangin' open. Get a couple of horses saddled. Move it!" Boomer had enough wind left in him to yell orders. "TJ! Hurry! You got to get Blue!"

"I'm going." He twisted, dragging Callie Mae with him, and found his mother bent over the wounded horseman, tears streaming down her cheeks. Emmett was nowhere in sight. "Stay with Boomer, Maggie. Get him to a doctor."

"Oh, God, TJ." By the looks of her, she was on the

verge of hysteria, her bosom heaving as she fought the demons she was never without. "I—I can't do this without you."

"You've got to take care of him. He needs you. There's no one else." TJ threw a frantic glance in the direction he'd last seen Blue, but there was no sign of his prized stallion. Nausea rolled through him. "Lodi will help."

The jockey trotted toward them with a pair of horses in tow. "Here you go, TJ."

Callie Mae made a sound of protest. "Let me go, damn you."

"Not a chance, darlin'. I'm not letting you out of my sight. Not until you listen to what I have to say." Keeping a good hold on her, he stuffed the derringer inside the waistband of his Levi's.

Her fingers clawed at his arm. "You can't make me go with you."

"The hell I can't." He took the reins Lodi thrust at him. "Climb in the saddle, or I'll throw you in it."

She tugged and pulled. "I'll escape you first chance I get."

His teeth gritted. She was high-handed and stubborn enough to do it. Under the circumstances, he couldn't blame her. But he was losing valuable time arguing with her, and he gripped her chin hard to keep her attention.

"Listen to me. You want the truth about what happened to Danny?" he demanded.

Her eyes flashed. "I already know it."

"No. You don't. But I'm going to find it. And you're

going to help me. But first, we have to get Blue. We have to get Blue." Of their own accord, his fingers softened against her chin. If he'd had the time to get down on his knees to beg her to understand, to convince her how much he needed her, needed her help, too, then he would.

"But Kullen—"

"He was part of it, Callie Mae," TJ said roughly. "Didn't what happened just now prove it?"

"No. You're wrong." But she appeared stricken at the possibility. "He would never—"

"Yes, he would." TJ took advantage of her hurt and confusion, and shoved the reins into her hands. Amazingly, she took them. "If Danny had to die, at least let him rest in the truth."

A faint shimmer of tears formed, a crumbling of her resistance.

"Lodi and my mother will see to Kullen," TJ persisted. Not that the bastard deserved the help, but TJ refrained from saying so. "And don't go fretting he needs you, because he doesn't. He's not the man you think he is. Everything that happened just now, he had coming."

She jerked an uneasy glance toward Kullen, whimpering like a baby in the dirt. She seemed to steel herself against the sight of him.

Then, as if she recalled she was a Lockett, that she carried the power of their blood in her veins, she stood a little taller. Turned a little tougher.

"I'll go with you, TJ, but I swear, if you're up to no good, I'll have you swinging from the gallows for this."

TJ drew in a breath of relief.

For now, it was enough.

He stepped back while she mounted up, then he did the same.

Together, they rode hard into the wilds of Texas to find Blue.

Chapter Four

By the time dusk showed signs of settling on the horizon, Callie Mae knew she'd made a big mistake.

Taking off with TJ Grier, of all people. Riding as if her tail was on fire, to chase a horse who had fled to only God knew where.

What had she been thinking?

She should have taken the time to sort the matter through and consider the consequences of all that had happened back at Preston Farm. The claims TJ had made. Kullen's actions, especially.

But everything had happened chillingly fast. Too fast to comprehend. She never expected Kullen to draw a gun, and then a knife…

He would've killed TJ.

The certainty troubled her. She didn't know why he hated TJ so much, enough to shoot him in cold blood. The things he said about TJ's continued involvement in horse racing, well, in spite of everything, they weren't worth killing him over.

Kullen had a heap of explaining to do. Maybe he was only acting in her best interests, prepared to fight for Tres Pinos. Or maybe he was trying to defend her against anything TJ might have done. Or defend himself.

Whatever his reasons for pulling that gun, she had to find out what they were. Which meant she shouldn't have left with TJ. She was Kullen's intended, and he was badly injured, in need of a surgeon. She should be at his side, caring for him, instead of being all the way out here, in the middle of the desolate Texas Panhandle, looking for a horse they had no chance of finding.

"Pull up, Callie Mae."

She bristled at TJ's low command. She had to end this wild-goose chase before they went any farther. She'd all but lost her bearings anyway, and she had no desire to head back toward Amarillo in the dark.

Gladly, she reined in. "This is ridiculous, TJ. You're not going to find him."

"Your opinion. Not mine." The grim clench of his jaw revealed that his mind was wrapped on his horse. He ran a slow eye over the land before them. An unforgiving land, rough with mesquite and pinon and looking more imposing than ever in the gathering dusk.

"It could take weeks," she said.

"Not if I can help it."

"Or months."

"Doesn't matter. I'm going to keep looking." His hard glance swiveled toward her. "And so are you."

He wore the brim of his Stetson low over his forehead, throwing the rugged, angular planes of his face into shadow. Ruthlessness shimmered from him. A brutal kind of determination that sent an unexpected thrum through her blood.

Her fingers tightened on the reins. She refused to let him affect her. "Do you really believe you can tell me what I am and am not going to do?"

His expression darkened with the warning that he'd have no tolerance for any resistance she was inclined to make. "You're the reason I'm out here, Callie Mae. I'd still have my horse if you hadn't ridden out to Boomer's, flaunting your high-and-mighty Lockett airs and making demands I have no intention of meeting."

"My fault?" Aghast, she stared at him. "I do *not* have airs, damn you. I simply rode out to discuss a business matter. And you've no right to say it was my fault that—"

She halted. Realized he'd backed her into a corner. If she hadn't been so determined to negotiate with him for Tres Pinos Valley, chaos wouldn't have erupted and they wouldn't be out here now, pursuing a racehorse that meant nothing to her, but clearly meant the world to TJ.

But she couldn't have known Kullen would've acted like he did. Not for a single moment in her lifetime.

He conspired against Danny, Callie Mae. He's responsible for everything that happened that night.

TJ's terse claim thundered back into her mind. Left her shaken and confused all over again. TJ had pulled the trigger and felled her brother; he'd admitted it again and again. How could he say Kullen was involved?

He's not the man you think he is.

"You owe it to me to help figure out why things happened the way they did at Boomer's," TJ said, as if he knew the way of her thoughts. "And it's a fair guess, when we do, we're going to see they had something to do with Danny."

The words to argue lodged in her throat. She didn't want to consider there might be a thread of truth in his words. That Kullen's actions proved something dark and elusive happened the night Danny died.

It was far easier to hang on to her resentment at being forced into this pursuit. She'd find her own way to learn if secrets shrouded her brother's death. She didn't need TJ to help her do it.

Callie Mae straightened in the saddle. "You're wrong in thinking I owe you anything, TJ. Even if there was a remote chance you're right about Kullen, the fact remains, you shot him and left him behind to fend for himself."

TJ grunted. "Shooting was too good for him."

She gritted her teeth against his lack of remorse. "He needs me. I must see to his welfare."

"Let Maggie and Lodi tend to him."

Her frustration grew. "I can't just run off with you, TJ. My parents are in California, and I have responsibilities at the C Bar C. The outfit will worry if I'm not there."

"We'll send word to 'em." He squinted an eye, returned his scrutiny to the endless terrain stretching in front of them. "You seem to have forgotten it was Kullen who drew his gun first, Callie Mae. He had every intention of killing me—and Boomer, too. What happened to him back there, he deserved."

She pressed her lips together against the harshness of TJ's logic, but she could find no argument with which to retaliate. Kullen's actions were indeed troubling. There was no sense to them.

"He's working with Emmett," TJ added roughly.

She hid her surprise with a frown. "Who?"

"My groomer." He turned back toward her, the line of his jaw hard, the sheen in his eyes like flint. "Emmett Ralston. He came to work for me a few weeks ago, and he's been feeding Kullen information ever since."

Callie Mae shivered at the revelation—and at the fury TJ could barely contain. She supposed he directed some of it at himself for being duped; the rest, well, blood would spill when he saw Emmett Ralston again.

"The man is your problem. Not mine. Whatever association Kullen has with him, I'll determine after I see to his welfare." Resolutely, she tugged on the reins. "I've changed my mind about this crazy chase, TJ. I'm heading back to Amarillo."

But before she could turn her mount, TJ's arm shot out and he grabbed firm hold on the bridle.

"The hell you will," he growled. "You're staying with me."

She smacked his forearm. "Let go!"

His grasp only tightened. "You're not *safe* with him, Callie Mae."

She drew back in frustrated exasperation. "That's ridiculous. Of course, I am."

"You're a fool to trust him farther than you can spit, and if you don't believe that, then you're not nearly as smart as you should be. Didn't what happened at Boomer's tell you anything?"

He's not the man you think he is...you think he is...you think he is...

The warning echoed again in her mind.

She fought it back into silence. Kullen was one of the most intelligent, kind, loyal men she'd ever known. He loved her. He'd told her so many times over. He'd never do anything to hurt her.

She leveled TJ with an imperious look, letting her contempt for his accusations show.

"He'll be my husband soon. I trust him more than anyone," she said.

TJ released the bridle and sat back, glaring at her. His lip curled. "Your husband."

"Not that it's any of your business."

A mask of indifference fell across his shadowed features. "You could marry the devil for all I care, Callie Mae. But you agreed to come with me to find Blue and the truth about Danny's death. I mean to hold you to both."

He appeared ruthlessly determined, and desperation flickered inside her. "I have to go back to Amarillo. Kullen needs me."

"Don't pride yourself." TJ's demeanor turned frosty, and her skin chilled. "I always thought the

Lockett word meant something. Leastways, it did with your mother."

She stiffened at the barb.

"Guess I was wrong about you," he said.

At that moment, she despised him more than ever.

"Going to be hard to prove yourself in this world if you don't do what you say you're going to do."

How could he know that proving herself had become all-important, especially in her mother's absence? And was there really more to learn about Danny's death, as he claimed?

Her resistance crumbled. Damn him for leaving her defenseless against his attack. Danny would always be her one weak spot...

"Fine," she grated. Her questions to Kullen would have to wait; she fervently hoped he received the medical attention he needed without her. "I'll keep looking for your horse, but only for a little longer." She refused to look at TJ and told herself she was doing the right thing and that any suspicions hovering over her brother's death took priority over her concern for Kullen.

Didn't they?

A headache stirred. She threw a scowling look around her. "Where are we anyway?"

A moment passed. Callie Mae could feel him watching her, his gaze pulling, but she quelled the urge to meet it. She sensed there was more he intended to say, yet his silence indicated he'd thought better of it.

"Just inside the Potter County line. Not far from the eastern boundary of the C Bar C," he said.

His voice had lost its edge. Was he relieved some of the fight had drained from her? That she intended to cooperate with him?

Had his worry for her been that deep?

"A friend of mine lives over there." He lifted a long arm and pointed toward a stand of pines in the distance. Dingy smoke curling in the darkening sky indicated a cabin hidden somewhere beyond them. "Might be he's seen Blue."

TJ urged his horse forward. Resigned, Callie Mae followed.

TJ rarely lied. In fact, he never did—except once in recent memory. But telling Callie Mae he could care less about who she married was as bald-faced a lie as a man could tell.

He did care. More than he should.

More than he had a right.

Her choice of husbands was none of his business, but damn it, what was she thinking? They didn't come any shiftier than Kullen Brosius. And she couldn't be more blind not to see it.

That scared the hell out of him—Callie Mae being blind. It meant Kullen had fooled her but good. It meant she'd fight TJ like a she-cat if he tried to prove her thinking wrong.

And that's just what he intended to prove, whether she liked it or not. To keep her from making the biggest mistake of her life.

Grimly, he skirted the grouping of pine trees, and

the faint crunch of hooves against fallen needles assured him she wasn't far behind. He didn't know how long he'd be able to keep her with him. She could turn and bolt the minute his back was turned, and what would he do then? Tear after her? When he had to find Blue first?

God, but he hoped he didn't have to make the choice. The stallion could be miles away in who knew which direction, and it might take days, weeks, to hunt him down. He couldn't expect Callie Mae to endure it, and yet—

She drew up beside him, and he halted.

And yet, he wanted her to do just that.

TJ allowed himself to be reminded of how beautiful she was, her body slender inside a tan checked gown trimmed in gold-and-brown silk. She sat in the saddle with her shoulders square, her back straight. She looked every bit a Lockett sitting there. Every bit female. And the blood in his groin stirred.

He hadn't ridden with her in years. Not since they were kids, when he was a gangly wrangler who couldn't get a string of words out in her presence without twisting his tongue around them first. She was five years younger and off-limits as the boss's daughter. She'd grown up knowing him as just another sun-browned face in the crowded C Bar C outfit, and TJ had had to work hard to keep from wearing his heart on his sleeve.

"Who lives here?" she asked.

He dragged his thoughts back from the past and regretted how her question was a reminder of why they were here. Of how everything had changed the night Danny died. That she'd always despise him because of what Kullen had done.

Which only proved all the more that he had to find Blue and satisfy his revenge.

TJ's gaze joined Callie Mae's on the small log cabin nestled amongst the pines. Their horses stood on the edge of a yard overrun with weeds and dotted with spots of bare ground. A light shone through a thin curtain covering one of the windows.

"His name's Dale Cooper. He worked for your mother a while back," he said.

"Stinky Dale?"

She swiveled toward him in surprise, and for once, there was no animosity in her expression.

Again, the sight of her distracted him. The wide-brimmed contrivance she called a hat darkened her face, yet silhouetted its regal shape. The wind had pulled at her hair, and wisps fluttered against her temple and cheeks. A large ostrich feather lay askew on top; a wide brown-and-gold-striped bow needed straightening. Damned if he knew how she managed to keep the thing on her head, even if they hadn't been riding hell-bent for leather across the Texas range.

"TJ." A hint of impatience lent a snap to her voice. "I asked you—*Stinky* Dale?"

His brain scrambled off her and back onto the name she demanded he clarify. Hell, she probably thought he was an idiot.

"Yes." TJ returned his scrutiny to the cabin and refused to let her distract him again. "He left the C Bar C when he bought this section of land. Got married and had a couple of kids."

"I remember him." She sounded defensive, as if he thought she wouldn't.

"You should. He was a good cowboy. Spent his growing-up years on your ranch."

Callie Mae sniffed. "By the looks of this place, he should never have left."

TJ was inclined to agree, but he kept his mouth shut. A man couldn't be blamed for wanting a spread of his own; some just did a better job than others at having one.

"You'll know his wife," he said instead. "Becky Rupp."

A moment passed—her brain working, he guessed, to place the name.

"Her father, Ben Rupp, keeps sheep down by Childress Way," he added to poke her memory.

She shifted in the saddle, as if impatient with his prodding. "I don't recall the name."

For some reason, that annoyed him. As a Lockett, she should be familiar with the ranchers and farmers in the area, something her mother had always made a point of doing.

Most likely, she'd been too busy cavorting with the likes of Kullen Brosius, living her carefree high-society life while everyone else toiled for their living, clinging to dreams that could shatter when they least expected it.

Someone like himself.

Glowering, he nudged his horse toward Stinky Dale's cabin, and this time, TJ didn't bother to check if Callie Mae followed.

Chapter Five

~~~~~~~~~~~~~~~~~

The cabin door opened, and Stinky Dale stepped out in his stocking feet. The aroma of frying potatoes wafted from behind him. He peered into the dusk.

"Well, I'll be damned," he said in surprise. "That you, TJ?"

"It is." TJ drew up, crossed his wrists over the saddle horn and tried to look calmer than he felt. "Hope you don't mind us showing up at your doorstep like this."

"Hell, no." The cowboy's gaze swung toward Callie Mae. "Who's that you got with you?"

"Callie Mae Lockett."

A moment passed. "You don't say."

She shifted, and the angle of her head showed more of her face beneath the wide brim. "Hello, Stinky."

"Miss Lockett." The cowboy stood a little straighter, his stance showing the respect he'd always had for her and her parents. "You're all growed up now, aren't you?"

"It was inevitable, I suppose." She gave him a small smile.

TJ cleared his throat. Social niceties weren't going to help him find his horse, but before he could open his mouth to ask about Blue, a woman appeared in the doorway.

Stinky's wife, Becky. By the looks of the plain-looking dress hanging on her thin frame, times were hard for them. She dried her hands on flour-sack toweling and swept a curious glance over them.

"Who're you talking to out here, Dale?" she asked.

"TJ Grier. He's got Callie Mae Lockett with him."

"Grier?" She stilled, looking alarmed. "Isn't he the one—"

"Yes." Stinky Dale's mouth went tight.

And TJ should've known the mistake he'd make in coming. Of course, Stinky Dale and Becky had heard about Danny's death. They would've heard about TJ's part in it, too, just like everyone had, not only in the Texas Panhandle, but in surrounding states and beyond.

Except TJ had thought Stinky Dale would be different. That he wouldn't believe. They'd spent too many years together on the C Bar C, sweating and swearing, wrangling horses and punching cows, for the wiry cowboy to think TJ was capable of the crime.

But from the grim look on Stinky Dale's face, TJ thought wrong.

He steeled himself against burning hurt. Chastised himself for the weakness. Consoled himself with the knowledge he didn't need Stinky Dale or his tired-looking wife to find Blue. He didn't need anyone. And the longer he sat there, enduring their stares and high-handed judgments, the longer it'd take to prove to them he wasn't a killer.

A child-killer.

Damn them all to hell.

He slammed his gaze into Callie Mae's.

"Let's go," he grated.

He hadn't known she was staring at him, too. Condemning him like the Coopers were? Blaming him? Hating him for all that had happened?

He cursed the dusk and the shadows that hid her face beneath the hat brim. He didn't like not knowing what was inside her head, the thoughts that were certain to be on the past. On him. That gave her the advantage, and he'd about had his limit from being on the wrong end of it.

"Not yet, TJ," she said, not moving.

Her tone held the same firm command he'd heard often enough from Carina, her mother, the she-boss he'd once revered. Still would revere, if she hadn't banished him forever from the C Bar C.

"You had a reason for dragging me out to Stinky Dale's place this time of night," Callie Mae continued in a cool voice. "Now that we're here, go on and ask him what you need to know."

"I've changed my mind on it," he said tersely.

"Is that so?"

He didn't grace her challenge with a response, but yanked on the reins to turn his mount. He refused to argue with her, with Stinky Dale and Becky being witness. The horse pranced, ready to run, but a tiny part of TJ, the disgustingly weak part of him, wasn't ready to leave yet.

Not without asking about Blue.

Callie Mae huffed an exasperated breath and turned to the Coopers.

"He's looking for a horse," she said in brisk explanation. "A stallion. Thoroughbred. Three-years-old or thereabouts. Black as night and still wearing his lead rope."

Stinky Dale's glance jumped from her to TJ and back again. "A thoroughbred?"

"That's right," she said.

TJ would've been impressed at her recall if he hadn't been so damned annoyed with her. He tugged on the reins again, this time bringing himself back around to face her.

"You'll not be doing my talking for me, Callie Mae," he growled.

"Someone has to," she said. "You're sitting there, stiff as a stone wall."

"Can't imagine you losin' a thoroughbred," Stinky Dale drawled, clearly skeptical.

TJ snapped a glower at the cowboy. "I didn't lose him. He was spooked. On purpose."

"Yeah?"

"Have you seen him?" Callie Mae asked.

Stinky Dale shook his head. "No, but there's a lot of country out here."

Of which TJ didn't need to be reminded. Fear stirred in him anew. The worry he'd never see Blue again.

"Whereabouts was he runnin' from?" Stinky Dale asked.

"Preston Farm." TJ peered out into the darkening twilight and hoped against foolish hope that his horse would suddenly appear. Like magic.

"Boomer's place?" The cowboy appeared taken aback.

But, of course, Blue wouldn't appear. Magic would be too easy, and when had TJ's life been that?

"Yep." He gripped the reins. "We've taken up enough of your time, Stinky Dale. Go on back inside. Your supper's waiting." He braced himself for a long night of riding. Of relentless searching. "Come on, Callie Mae. Let's go."

Before he could turn his horse to leave, he encountered Becky Cooper's stare. The look in her face, the wide-eyed apprehension that shone through the shadows, chilled his blood.

She was afraid of him.

It was there in the way she held herself, stiff and wary. As if she was ready to bolt into the cabin and lock the doors tight if he so much as looked at her wrong.

What did she think he'd do? Hurt her?

The realization stunned him.

Because of what he'd done. What she *thought* he'd done, and how could he convince her he wasn't the monster she believed him to be?

The door burst open with a screech of its hinges. A

slick-haired boy of about four strode out. "Ma? When are we gonna eat?"

Another boy, a year younger, followed, but stopped short at the sight of visitors. "Hey, Pa! Who's here?"

He took an exuberant step toward Stinky Dale, but Becky gasped and moved faster, grabbed him by the collar and held him close. As if on second thought, she grabbed her oldest son, too, and pulled them both up against her.

"Stay here, boys," she commanded.

TJ didn't move. Didn't think. He could barely breathe from the insult.

"Becky." Stinky Dale frowned the warning.

"You know what he did, Dale," she said, her voice unsteady. "We have to be careful." She stood taller, her thin face resolute in the dimming light, and leveled TJ with a condescending glance. "We haven't seen your horse, Mr. Grier, like my husband said. So you'd best just ride on out of here and look for him somewhere else."

"I'll do that." TJ gathered his pride and wondered what had possessed him to think that stopping by Stinky Dale's was a good idea. "Sorry to have bothered you."

"Not so fast, TJ." Callie Mae's lips curved. "I'm rather glad we stopped here. In fact, I think I'd like to stay a while."

And with that, she swept aside her skirts, swung a leg over the saddle and dismounted.

* * *

"What are you doing, Callie Mae?"

TJ glowered down at her from the saddle. She had to tilt her head to glower right back at him.

"I doubt you've noticed, but it's getting dark. Cold, too. The horses are tired. They need to rest." She set her hands on her hips. "We have no food, no water, and I'm not going one step further."

"You knew this wasn't going to be a pleasure ride," he said, the rumble in his voice giving fair warning he'd throttle her if he could reach her.

"I'm not going to let it be a foolish one."

"She's right, TJ. You have to stop sometime. Reckon you can't find a horse you can't see." Stinky Dale cleared his throat. He seemed to make a pointed effort to avoid looking at his wife. "Come on in and have supper with us. You can stay the night and take off first thing in the morning."

"Dale!" Becky appeared appalled.

Callie Mae stiffened at the woman's rudeness. The way she clutched her sons tighter, especially.

Becky knew about the despicable crime he'd committed, of course. Clearly, she was terrified by it. Callie Mae couldn't blame her for not wanting TJ in her sights. What mother would?

But it couldn't be helped. Circumstances being what they were, Callie Mae had a strong need to partake of the Coopers' hospitality.

"We'd be much obliged for your kindness, Becky," she said, then halted when she heard with her own ears how the appeal sounded. Like she'd tucked her pride in her pocket to ask for help from this family who clearly had little to share.

When before had she had to lower herself?

Had she ever?

Well, as much as she disliked being on the receiving end of someone's assistance when her own wealth and abilities were formidable, she had to do what she could to get herself back to Amarillo and Kullen.

And she wasn't above using the Coopers to do it.

"Go on, Becky," Stinky Dale commanded, gesturing toward the door.

"I'd like a word with you first, Dale," she said firmly. "Inside."

The woman's reluctance had Callie Mae clutching what was left of her patience. She refused to stand there and beg when she'd already expressed her appreciation for their courtesy. Did Becky really expect her to wait like a meek little puppy while the couple argued the matter in private?

Callie Mae swung her skirt hems and strode toward the cabin door herself, despite the other woman's faint gasp of surprise. Callie Mae pulled the door open and held it wide, but stopped short of walking right in.

"We are an inconvenience, aren't we?" Her lips curved downward in demure regret. "I do apologize, but surely you understand our predicament?"

She held center stage among them all, even the pair of young boys who gaped at her in open-mouthed curiosity. Becky seemed at a loss for words, as did her husband, and yet it was TJ's stiff silence that affected Callie Mae most.

The bit of light from inside the cabin failed to illuminate his dark shape astride his horse. Failed to give her a hint of his thinking, too, but she could feel his humiliation as if it shot flames at her.

Something stirred inside her chest. She couldn't put a name to the feeling, but it was an uncomfortable one so she didn't try. He'd made it plain he wanted no part of staying at the Coopers'. She intended to ignore his demand. One of them needed to use the sense they were born with, didn't they? If he decided to leave without her, well, so much the better.

She pulled her gaze off TJ and found a bright smile for Becky.

"Let's go inside, shall we?" Callie Mae kept her voice smooth, coaxing, and opened the door even wider. "I assure you, our stay here won't be long."

Becky's dismayed glance flitted over her husband before she squared her shoulders with a nod. "All right." She nudged her sons forward. "Go on in, boys."

She followed them into the cabin without a glance at Callie Mae when she passed. Callie Mae didn't much care. Once they parted ways in the morning, she doubted she'd see Becky Cooper again, at least not for a good while.

Callie Mae went inside and pulled the door closed behind her. The simplicity of the cabin smacked into her resolve and sent it teetering. Small, sparsely furnished, the place contained only the main room and a curtained partition, behind which, she assumed, was the couple's bed. A pair of tiny cots had been tucked in the eaves above, and the crude ladder they needed to get up there stood in a corner.

The entire structure could fit inside Callie's Mae's bedroom back at the C Bar C. If she included her sitting room, that is. How could a family of four live in such tiny quarters?

Becky turned toward her.

"I don't believe we've been introduced proper, Miss Lockett," she said. Twin spots of pink colored her cheeks. Had she known what Callie Mae was thinking? She extended her hand. "My name is Becky Cooper."

"Hello, Becky. Please call me Callie Mae."

The woman's slender fingers felt rough as a boar's bristles. Becky kept her clasp brief, as if she was all too aware of it.

"These here are my boys, Stevie and Joel." She took a small step back, allowing Callie Mae to see them better.

"Hello, boys," Callie Mae said, noting how much they looked like Stinky Dale with their nutty brown hair slicked down and freckles scattered over their noses.

Danny had had freckles, too, when he was their age, she suddenly recalled. They'd disappeared as he got older, when his skin learned to tan, and his features showed signs he would grow up to be a handsome young man…

A dizzying rush of sadness assaulted her. She hated how the grief came when she least expected it. How it had the ability to nearly knock her to her knees. She drew in a breath and fought the sadness down.

"Are you really a Lockett?" Stevie, the older of the pair, stared up at her, clearly awed by the possibility.

"I am." Callie Mae dragged herself out of the grief and channeled her concentration on the boy, allowing herself to be distracted by his four-year-old innocence.

"Do you live on the C Bar C, too?" he asked.

She nodded, but an image of her prized Tres Pinos Valley popped into her mind. The home place she wanted for her very own. She'd have it, too, if it wasn't for that damn TJ.

"That's my family's ranch, yes," she said.

"My pa used to work there." Joel spoke up for the first time, but overwhelmed by a sudden burst of shyness, he grinned and buried his face in Becky's skirts. Her hand found the top of his head, and she held him gently against her.

"I remember," Callie Mae said, amused.

"I'm gonna work there, too, when I'm growed up." Stevie, clearly the braver of the two, declared. "Just like my pa."

"We'd be proud to have you." Callie Mae spoke with utmost seriousness for the boy's sake. "He was a fine cowboy when he worked for us."

"Are you gonna have supper here?" Joel asked, peeping at her.

Her gaze moved to him. "Would that be all right?"

"Yeah." He buried his face again.

Callie Mae's gaze kept moving toward the wooden

table which occupied a good portion of the living area. Four plates lay neatly on top; beside them, four forks. All in readiness for the meal the Coopers had been ready to eat.

In the center sat a bowl of fried potatoes; next to it, a plate holding a piece of sliced beef. A cast-iron skillet waited on one of the stove's burners, reminding Callie Mae how her arrival with TJ had interrupted Becky's preparations.

"Is there anything I can do to help you finish making supper?" Callie Mae asked.

"It's finished." Becky kept her glance direct, though her small swallow revealed what it cost her to admit it. "You're not stayin' at the C Bar C, Miss Lockett."

Unwittingly, Callie Mae's gaze returned to that lone piece of meat, that inadequate bowl of potatoes, meant to feed four mouths.

Now, with hers and TJ's, they'd have to feed two more.

Callie Mae's brain scrambled for the words to redeem herself for the mistake she'd made. To appear less selfish in someone's eyes who clearly believed that Callie Mae had more than she could ever need. Maybe more than she deserved.

She failed.

As if she knew her point had been taken, Becky shifted her attention to her children, saving Callie Mae from the indignity of having to defend herself for having the privileges that came from being a Lockett.

"Go on and wash up, boys. We'll eat as soon as

your father comes in." Her glance flitted back to Callie Mae. "You might as well do the same. I'll find a clean towel for you." But before she left, her gaze reluctantly lifted, reminding Callie Mae of how windblown she must look with the tendrils of hair that had escaped from beneath the brim of her hat while she chased after TJ's horse.

Wistfulness crossed Becky's expression.

"You have mighty fine taste in millinery, Miss Lockett," she said softly. Then, as if she'd revealed too much, the wistfulness disappeared, and she strode toward a pine chest for the towel she'd promised.

Callie Mae caught her reflection in a small mirror hanging above an enamel basin of water. The glass could barely hold her image, the brim of her hat being so wide, the brown-and-gold striped bow outrageously flamboyant, the frothy ostrich feather blown crooked. The cabin's lantern light failed to glamorize her dress, too. The tan checks appeared dull, the silk trimming insignificant.

Never had Callie Mae felt so out of place.

She looked it, too.

No wonder Becky resented her.

Had it been only this afternoon that Callie Mae had enjoyed a lavish dinner at the Amarillo Hotel? With succulent roast beef and asparagus, with a dessert so rich she couldn't finish it? Surrounded by the smells of expensive imported cigars and brandy in crystal glasses on starched tablecloths, enjoying the company of men who made more money in a week than Stinky Dale could hope to make in an entire year?

Her meeting with the prominent entrepreneurs determined to build an exposition on her land.

TJ Grier and his damned horse had yanked her out of her high-society world with all its frivolity and responsibilities. He'd plunked her into his desperate one with no thought of all he'd forced her to leave behind.

And then there was Kullen.

The truths she needed to find about Danny, too.

She bit her lip. And now, here she was, taking food from a family who could barely make ends meet.

Maybe she should've listened to TJ, after all...

How was this all going to end?

Chapter Six

TJ glared at the closed door. The irritation built in him that Callie Mae had taken matters into her own hands and helped herself to the hospitality Stinky Dale offered without a care for what TJ wanted. She'd left him behind, still in the saddle and damn near shaking from frustration.

Now what was he supposed to do?

"She always was a hard one to hold down," Stinky Dale said, watching him. "Like smoke in a bottle."

TJ grunted. That about covered it. Smoke in a bottle. From the time he'd known her, Callie Mae had been like that. Elusive. Out of his reach. Untouchable.

Time only made it worse. His troubles after Danny's death, being thrown in jail, his reputation ruined, hell, she was more out of his reach than ever. Damned if he could see things changing anytime soon.

"Slide down off that horse, TJ, and cool your saddle for a spell." Stinky Dale pulled out a rolled cigarette, rooted for a match next. "We got some catchin' up to do."

TJ knew he expected an explanation. Figured he was entitled to one, besides. TJ couldn't leave without Callie Mae, though it'd serve her right if she had to fend for herself out here. Truth was, he didn't want her out of his sight. He needed her too much.

Chasing after Blue was going to have to wait. He consoled himself with the knowledge the stallion couldn't run all night any more than they could, but still feeling grim over it, TJ dismounted. Stinky Dale struck the match and lit a lantern hanging on a rusty nail, then stroked the match flame against the end of his cigarette. Wordlessly, he handed the quirley to TJ and lit a second.

The cowboy squatted on his haunches in the grass. TJ joined him, drew in deep on the tobacco and exhaled slow. He lifted his hat and ran a tired hand through his hair before settling the Stetson back onto his head.

The lantern light revealed his old friend hadn't changed much. Still wore his hair slicked down with some kind of bear grease. Still wore the cologne that smelled like a bad mix of spices. Still had skin tanned and lined from the sun, hands rough from hard work.

Just like when they wrangled together on the C Bar C. A lifetime ago.

Only a few years older than TJ, Stinky Dale had moved on since those days. Bought his own place, made himself a family. TJ had nothing—except one beautiful horse.

Now he didn't even have that.

He squinted an eye over the dark horizon and fought the pain from it. Silence fell. Familiar. Oddly comforting. Stinky Dale was being patient, but TJ sensed his reservations, the questions he needed to ask.

Once, TJ could've trusted Stinky Dale with the truth he kept locked tight inside. Could he still? Or would the cowboy be suspicious? Resentful, like his wife?

"She's got supper waiting for you," TJ said quietly.

"Talkin's more important right now."

TJ nodded, but still the words wouldn't come. Blamable pride, he supposed, that had him nursing some resentment of his own that the cowboy could believe him capable of the crime he paid dearly for.

"Reckon Becky's packing a grudge against you," Stinky Dale said, rubbing his chin. "Guess I ought to apologize for that."

"Don't," TJ said. He hadn't appreciated her behavior, but he could understand it.

"Those boys mean the world to her."

"They should."

Stinky Dale blew out a breath. "It's just that folks have been speculating about you, TJ, and—"

"Doesn't mean I'd hurt anyone," he said roughly. "Do you really think I would?"

"You 'fessed up to the crime that killed Danny McClure, didn't you?" he shot back. "That *tells* me you would."

TJ clamped his mouth shut, and the decision he'd made back then tore through him. A thousand times, a million, he'd questioned the wisdom of what he'd done.

The cabin door swung open, and Stinky Dale's oldest popped his head out.

"Hey, Pa. You comin' in to eat?" he demanded.

Stinky Dale stayed hunkered. "Tell your ma to start without me, son. I'll be in directly."

"Okay." The door slammed shut again.

TJ stayed hunkered, too.

"Fine-looking boy," he said, trying for a change of subject. A safer one, at least. "Both of them are."

"So how in blazes did you get within spittin' distance of Callie Mae tonight without her burnin' some powder on you?" Stinky Dale demanded, unswayed.

"I didn't give her a choice." TJ frowned, remembering.

"Yeah?" Stinky Dale looked skeptical.

"I put a gun to her head."

Even now he couldn't believe he'd done it.

"Jesus, TJ," Stinky said, staring.

"I know."

His gaze lifted to the cabin window. He found her, framed within the panes, her attention held by something Stevie was telling her while they sat at the table, eating supper.

She'd taken off her hat, and the room's golden light glinted on her hair, turning the strands a rich shade of cinnamon. She wore the mass swept back and piled into a loose roll on her head, making him curious about its thickness, its weight, how it would feel sliding through his fingers. If all that glorious hair had become too heavy for its pins.

His gaze tarried on the wisps that had escaped and curled against her temple, her cheek. A result of their ride, he knew. Fast and frantic from Boomer's. TJ had a strong longing to smooth those wayward strands from her face and tell her how much he regretted being forced to do what he'd done.

How desperate he'd become.

To find Blue. To find the truth.

To keep her with him, so he could.

"Guess you forgot who she was when you held that gun to her head, didn't you?" Stinky Dale accused softly.

TJ pulled himself out of his thoughts, like a boot from sticky mud.

"Callie Mae?" he asked.

"She's a *Lockett,* TJ." Stinky stressed the word, as if TJ had never heard it before. "She's got more power in her little finger than you and me will ever have our whole lives." He let the words soak in. "When she gets that inheritance her grandma left her, she'll have more money than just about everyone else, too."

"You think I give a damn about any of those things?"

Stinky's lips thinned. "Reckon you never did, least-ways when we wrangled together on the C Bar C. But you should." He took a quick puff off his cigarette. "Besides, you spent time in jail for killin' her brother. You for sure didn't forget *that* when you put a gun to her, did you?"

TJ glowered. Had he ever heard a question more ridiculous? "No, Stinky. I didn't."

"Why'd you do it, then?"

"Because she's being duped and doesn't know she is, that's why. And I was framed for Danny's death," he blurted.

Stinky Dale went still. Smoke curled from the end of his quirley, and he squinted through the hazy swirls.

"You tellin' me there's more to the story?" he asked.

"A hell of a lot more."

But once the words were out, TJ turned hesitant. Except for Boomer and Maggie, he'd never voiced his suspicions that Kullen Brosius was somehow responsible for what happened to Danny with anyone but Sheriff Dunbar and Harvey Whelan, the only lawmen he dared to confide in. It'd been a good long while since he'd seen Stinky Dale. TJ wasn't sure he could still be trusted—or would believe anything TJ had to say.

"I'll listen, if you want to talk," the cowboy said quietly.

TJ's defenses cracked. Stinky Dale always did have the ability to read his mind. Seemed the years hadn't changed that. Most times, he agreed with what TJ was thinking, which was how they'd gotten to be good friends.

TJ wanted to trust him and knew that Stinky Dale would listen to him now, when it mattered most. TJ needed to be assured he wasn't crazy.

Even if it seemed he was.

"The night Danny died, Carina and Penn threw a party for Callie Mae." He figured the beginning was the best place to start. "She'd been in Europe for a spell, and they wanted to welcome her home."

The cowboy nodded. "Folks from all over these parts was talkin' about that party. You'd a thought the president of the United States was comin' to visit."

TJ recalled the talk, too. The preparations. The hoopla. How the most prominent of the Panhandle's citizenry had been invited.

"Someone at the party told Danny I wanted to see him. So he slipped away without anyone knowing and set out to find me at the new horse barn."

"'Someone,'" Stinky said. "You don't know who?"

"No. Except that it was a woman."

TJ had lain awake nights trying to figure out who she was. Why she would've lied to the boy. Who she was working with, most of all.

"I had no reason to go through her to leave a message for Danny, especially at that late hour," TJ said. "I could've talked to him any time of day I wanted."

The cowboy nodded. "You could." He studied the burning tip of his cigarette, as if sorting through the story. "So this person wanted the boy there. Any idea why?"

"They meant to use him somehow."

Stinky's expression turned grim. "You figure they wanted to kidnap him? Hold him for ransom?"

"I'm figuring that, yes."

But TJ's gut said there was more. Something deeper. More menacing.

"The C Bar C is one of the biggest spreads in Texas." Stinky heaved a troubled sigh. "Easy to think they got greedy and wanted to hit Carina and Penn where it hurt most."

TJ's stomach clenched at how well they'd succeeded. "Damned shame they had to use an innocent child to do it."

Stinky Dale's gaze lifted. The lantern light failed to hide his suspicion or the confusion that put it there. "But you claimed to kill him. Why'd you shoot at him?"

"Whoever was waiting in that barn tried to run, but Danny—he got in the way." The words sent shards of pain and regret into TJ's chest. "It was an accident, Stinky," he said roughly. "An *accident*."

"The judge and jury didn't think so."

"They were bought. And they didn't waste time convicting me of involuntary manslaughter." God, he detested the charge, the ugliness of the words.

"Folks trust the law in this country." The cowboy's gaze didn't waver. "So that's a hell of an accusation, TJ. Not like you to make it unless you knew for sure." He regarded him. Hard. "Do you? Know for sure?"

"No." It galled him to make the admission. He refused to explain how little he knew, that he had to rely on instinct until he got the facts from either Harvey or the sheriff and hopefully both, and what did it matter if Stinky Dale believed him or not? TJ mashed the stub of his cigarette into the ground. Furiously. "The fire destroyed the barn, and if there was any evidence about the person waiting for him, it's gone. The judge heard nothing to prove I wanted to hurt Danny."

"Ah, but you're wrong, TJ."

He jerked toward the softly sarcastic voice behind him and found Callie Mae standing outside the door.

She took a leisurely step forward, yet the contemptuous arch of her brow revealed her disdain at the conversation she'd been eavesdropping.

He didn't know how much she'd heard, but she looked ready to tangle horns with him. He rose to face her, ready for the fight. Stinky Dale rose, too, his glance jumping wary between them.

"The hell I am, Callie Mae," TJ said.

She halted. "The jury had one piece of evidence, and that's all they needed to convict you."

Remembering, his lip curled. "That evidence should've proved that if I really wanted to kill Danny, which I didn't, I wouldn't have done it like it happened."

"You'd been drinking, and it was your shotgun that killed him, TJ. You admitted pulling the trigger. There's not clearer evidence than that."

"Whoa, you two." Stinky held up his hand. "What piece of evidence are you talking about?"

Callie Mae's throat moved in the lantern light, as if she had to try hard to keep her composure.

"A single shotgun pellet killed my brother, Stinky Dale," she said. "He died instantly. And—"

"It was a wild shot, Callie Mae," TJ grated. "Never intended for him. Never."

"Easy to say that now, isn't it?" she snapped. "When you're sober."

Remorse burned like bile in his stomach. Yes, he'd broken C Bar C rules by having a few beers that night. Hell, everyone there was guilty of doing the same thing. But he hadn't had so many that he couldn't remember each haunting detail of what happened.

"A hundred times I said it was an accident, but the judge didn't listen," he said.

And neither had she. Or her parents. TJ had Kullen Brosius to thank for that. The bastard had ruthlessly manipulated them all as if they were puppets on strings, and he had yet to fathom why Brosius was so determined to see him convicted.

But he would. One day soon.

"I've always known TJ to be an expert marksman," Stinky Dale said, looking as if he didn't know what to make of all he was hearing. "Once he eyed a target, with a shotgun—" He halted, cleared his throat, threw Callie Mae a stricken glance. "Not that he'd make Danny a target. No, ma'am. Hell, I just can't believe he would."

"Seems you're about the only one who can't," TJ said, knowing how self-pitying he sounded but unable to help himself. "Danny was as fine a boy as could be found. Everyone thought so."

"No, not everyone," Callie Mae said stiffly. "Or else he'd be alive today."

He detected the hurt in her voice, felt for himself the grief that still hovered raw and aching beneath her skin. He heard the blame she felt for him, too, which he didn't deserve but which he accepted, and if he never did anything else in his pathetic life, he intended to find out the truth and stamp his own brand of justice on whoever was responsible.

Yet the words to tell her as much stayed on his

tongue. She wasn't ready to listen yet. Or to believe. She wasn't willing to trust that he wanted answers, too, *needed* them as much as she did.

More, most likely.

She stood glaring up at him in the lantern's light. He couldn't recall the last time he was this close to her, not when she was the almighty Callie Mae Lockett and he was just another cowboy in the C Bar C outfit. He breathed different air than she did up there on her pedestal. Lived a whole different life. Leaving him with no choice but to admire her from afar.

To love her, too.

Most every cowboy in three surrounding states fancied himself in love with her one time or another, and he had nothing on any of them.

Not anymore.

TJ soaked in the privilege of being with her now. The shadowy light hid the color of her eyes, darkened the color of her hair, but he could see her weariness as plain as if she stood beneath the noonday sun.

He had to fist his hands to keep from touching her. She wouldn't appreciate his attempt to comfort. The glare lingering in her expression warned him as much, but the need in him was there. Growing. Making him forget about Stinky Dale and Blue and the terrible thing done to Danny that needed righting.

"I've changed my mind about staying here," she said coolly, sending his thoughts rippling. "I want to keep riding."

Her demand startled him. She'd been adamant about stopping for the night. As much as he wanted to comply, though, her fatigue concerned him, and he shook his head in refusal.

"It's late," he said. "It's best if we both rest up and get a fresh start in the morning."

Her determined gaze held his. "Are you going to keep bucking me every minute, TJ? Let's mount up."

He frowned at the impatience in her voice. Something had happened at supper, he suspected. With Becky? The boys?

"You're needin' that horse to help you find out what really happened to Danny, aren't you, TJ?" Stinky Dale asked, his tone pensive, his scrutiny shrewd. "That's why you're all-fired up to find him."

TJ dragged his glance from Callie Mae. He could almost feel the cowboy delving into his thoughts, reading them to understand. "That's right."

"How? You going to sell him?"

"No." The plans he'd made with Boomer, the hopes and dreams that might never happen if he didn't find his precious Blue, reared up in his mind all over again. "I'm going to race him."

Stinky's brows arched. "Race him!"

"Yes."

For the money he'd earn, TJ could do all he had to do to prove his innocence and undo the damage a shyster like Kullen Brosius had done. To get his life, his independence, his good name back.

Blue could do all those things for him, but he refrained from saying so. Callie Mae wouldn't agree to his methods, and he was of no mind to argue with her.

But a small smile of approval formed on Stinky Dale's mouth, telling TJ he didn't need to say a thing. "You two had better get a move on, then, hadn't you? Before that horse gets to runnin' too far."

"I'll just go in and get my hat." Callie Mae turned back toward the house, swishing her hems in her haste.

"Now hold on, Callie Mae," the cowboy said.

She halted. Swung toward him.

"You always did go for a lot of fancy riggin'—" he raked her gown with a pointed glance "—but you can't go traipsing all over the countryside dressed like you are."

She glanced down at her skirts. "Well, there's no help for it. I have nothing else."

"I'll find you something more fittin'. I'll fix you two up with some supplies, too. TJ, come on in and get some vittles while I do. You have any idea where you're going?"

TJ set his hands on his hips and scanned the darkness. Miles and miles of night-covered range. He swallowed and tried not to feel overwhelmed. "Not a one."

Stinky Dale reached around Callie Mae and opened the door, but he stopped before going in, as if a thought had just occurred to him. "Caught sight of a herd of mustangs today down by the Palo Duro. Runnin' wild and free, they was. Might be your horse caught up and decided to run with them for a spell."

Mustangs.

Blue was born with more spirit than a horse should

need. It was what TJ loved most about him, that spirit, and if Blue met up with a herd who thrilled on running, on freedom, as much as he did...

"If he's the horse you think he is," Callie Mae said quietly, her gaze steady. "He wouldn't be able to help himself."

Hope stirred in his blood. He hadn't expected her to share his thinking, but it seemed she did, and for now, it was enough.

It'd be a long shot, finding the herd of mustangs. Finding Blue with them, even longer.

But he had to try.

Chapter Seven

"What happened back there to make you so all-fired up to leave the Coopers?" TJ demanded.

Guided by the silvery moonlight, they'd ridden at a brisk pace from Stinky Dale's cabin toward the head of the Palo Duro Canyon, but the threat one of the horses could step into a prairie-dog hole or a rut hidden in the grass compelled TJ to slow down. Callie Mae had to admit she was glad for it. Every muscle in her body had begun to feel the hours he'd all but forced her to spend in the saddle.

"They barely had enough to eat for themselves," she said curtly. "Once I realized it, I couldn't expect them to feed us, too."

She'd stretched her serving of beef and potatoes by cutting them into small pieces and eating slowly. If Becky noticed, she didn't say anything. But then, the woman had been about as warm as an icicle. Callie Mae found it easiest to ignore her.

"Folks out here are accustomed to sharing what they have," TJ said. "Even if what they have isn't much."

"That doesn't mean I'm willing to take food from the mouths of children, and Becky made it plain she didn't like me much," Callie Mae retorted, annoyed she'd been made to defend herself. That he felt she needed educating, too. "I've lived in this part of Texas all my life. You make it sound as if I haven't."

"Maybe, but your life is different than most."

"Because I'm a Lockett?"

"Yep. C Bar C."

She regarded him from beneath the brim of the hat Becky had lent her. The darkness hid TJ's features, but she could feel the disapproval in him. She could see it, too, in the way he rode with the reins gripped in his fist, his back straight, his shoulders taut.

Was he angry with her? Blaming her for who she was?

Or merely consumed with finding his horse?

Some of all three, she suspected, and her regard lingered, held in place by the threads of awareness slipping through her veins, forcing her to acknowledge how he made an imposing figure silhouetted in the saddle. Rugged and virile.

Male.

She swiveled her head away and refused to keep looking at him. No denying he was all those things, but thinking of him as "virile," well, she couldn't let herself stray in that direction.

Even if he did have…appeal to him.

He was only a cowboy, she reminded herself firmly. A convicted one at that, and he'd caused her and her parents enough grief to last them a lifetime.

"My mother worked day and night for a good many years to build the C Bar C to the spread it is today, TJ," she said stiffly. "When she married Penn, he worked right along with her. They deserve every bit of the prosperity they've earned."

"Never said they didn't, and I'm glad they have it to enjoy." She could feel his glare but refused to meet it. "You forget I lived on the ranch, too. I know as well as anyone how hard they worked."

He'd been tireless in his own labors, she had to acknowledge. His devotion to the C Bar C, to her parents, had never been questioned.

Until the night Danny died.

Another round of weariness rolled through her, and she sighed. "Your point being?"

"That you've forgotten what it's like to be… average."

"Average?" Her brow arched. "How so?"

"That grandmother of yours, spoiling you from the time you figured what it meant, for starters."

"Hmm."

She had to concede him that. Mavis Webb never had a daughter of her own. Her son, Rogan—Callie Mae's no-good father—was killed a decade previous, victim of his own criminal activities. But even before then, Mavis had been as generous and devoted to Callie Mae as a grandmother could be.

More, most likely.

Callie Mae's spoiling had been a point of great contention between Mavis and Carina for years. For Callie Mae's sake, though, they'd managed to be polite to one another while she'd grown into full womanhood.

Now, sadly, Grandmother was gone, and as the last of the Webb bloodline, Callie Mae stood to inherit the formidable family fortune.

A daunting prospect, to say the least. Managing so much money in addition to the C Bar C's wouldn't be easy, but she'd have Kullen's help. His lawyerly advice would be invaluable. Already, they'd spent untold hours discussing their financial future after they were married.

A renewed wave of concern for him washed through her, and she bristled at the irony of how she'd abandoned him. And she refused to feel guilty for the advantages she'd been able to enjoy, both as a Lockett and a Webb.

"I was all the family Grandmother had," Callie Mae said, bringing herself back to TJ's comment and where she was—riding the range with him at an ungodly hour of night. "We loved each other very much."

"Which you should. I'm just saying not everyone is as privileged as you. Becky Cooper might think you don't know what it's like to have to work for an honest living. Or maybe she was embarrassed that she and Stinky Dale did."

If what he said was true, the woman would be wrong on both counts. Callie Mae grew up doing her share of chores. She'd gotten as sweaty and dirty as any of the C Bar C cowboys more times than she cared to count.

Except not so much anymore, Callie Mae had to admit, and that was likely the part Becky resented. Most days, Callie Mae traded her denims and boots for high-priced gowns and fine leather shoes. To attend parties and meetings with influential townsmen and politicians. To eat elegant foods and drink sparkling wines. All in the name of the C Bar C.

Business matters.

The scope of her responsibilities had changed, that's all.

And as far as Becky being embarrassed over what little she had, well, Callie Mae regretted she felt that way. There was no shame in raising a family and working a small spread. Callie Mae vowed to be a mite friendlier, to set the woman at ease, the next time she saw her.

TJ drew up then, and caught up in her thoughts, Callie Mae automatically followed suit. He rested his palms over the saddle horn.

"Speaking of privilege, Miss Lockett," he said in a low, mocking drawl. "When was the last time you spent the night in a bedroll?"

The seductiveness in his voice kicked at her imagination for what he might imply…until she assured herself he hadn't implied anything. Certainly nothing intimate. The question was a legitimate one.

"Not so long ago," she said, her chin lifting from her own foolishness.

"Back in '89, if I recall. Spring roundup. You woke up to find a snake coiled on top of your blanket. You damn near scared off the herd with your screaming."

"I didn't!"

Well, she might have shrieked a bit, but she deplored reptiles and was entitled. The disgusting creature kept her shuddering for weeks.

"Jesse Keller had to leave camp and take you all the way home," TJ added.

"He was very nice about it, too," she retorted.

Callie Mae had endured her share of teasing over the incident, but TJ was right. She hadn't spent a night outside since—and didn't regret it in the least.

"No one here to take you home tonight," TJ said and dismounted with the grace of a man who'd done it all his life. "It's too far, besides. So you'd best get down and we'll get ready to turn in."

He strolled toward her and got her imagination going. That intimacy again. The inevitability that the two of them would be together.

Sleeping.

Side by side.

We'll get ready to turn in...

"Now?" she asked and hated herself for it.

"Plenty late as it is."

She scrambled for her bearings and didn't move. "Where are we?"

"Miles from anywhere."

She'd known they'd have to stop eventually. They couldn't ride all night, and maybe she shouldn't have suggested leaving the Coopers, after all.

"What's the matter, Callie Mae? Don't want to sleep with me?" he taunted.

"Don't flatter yourself. I just wasn't ready to quit riding yet."

Not altogether true given the fatigue that had settled deep in her bones, but because he was waiting, she resolutely swung out of the saddle. In her denims, borrowed from Stinky Dale, it was a cinch; yet once on the ground, her stiff muscles protested, and she had to take a step back to steady herself.

TJ's hand quickly settled on her waist. The warmth of his palm touched her skin through the cotton of her shirt, and the strength in his fingers assured her she wasn't going to fall anytime soon.

"Easy," he said.

He must think her nothing but a silly, skittish female, but honestly, with him standing this close, tall and dark and broad-shouldered, her mind just up and cleared. She couldn't think of a thing to do—or say—but stand there and get used to him.

"Are you afraid of me?" he murmured, frowning.

Words of denial sprang onto her tongue. She held them in. He'd just given her an opportunity to gather her composure and make a thing or two understood.

"On the contrary, TJ." Her voice sounded flustered, in spite of her attempt to assert some authority over him, and she stood a little taller, so she could. "I quite enjoy the company of men. I find them fascinating and entertaining, most of the time." As a cattlewoman for the C Bar C, Callie Mae had grown accustomed to being the center of their attentions, whether for business or pleasure. "However, let me remind you

you're responsible for my brother's death. Witnesses will attest that I've been riding with you. Any harm done to me will most certainly lead to your hanging from the gallows."

His hand dropped from her waist, and he muttered a disgusted curse. "You really think I'd hurt you?"

"I never thought you'd hurt Danny, so your point is moot, isn't it?"

"I wouldn't, Callie Mae. Not ever." Anger shimmered from him, and he pivoted away. Then, he pivoted back. "I said what I did about Danny, but you're here with me because we both want the truth." He jabbed a finger at her, his control clearly precarious. "Until we get it, don't ever accuse me of hurting him again."

Looking as furious as he sounded, he strode away.

Callie Mae watched him go.

Well. It seemed she'd pushed him to the edge, but it had to be done. Who knew what he would do when she fell asleep and turned vulnerable?

Yet she remained rooted where she stood, her eyes staying on him while he moved past the horses to a clearing. And when she lost sight of him briefly, she shifted her stance a little, looking for him, then finding him, from over her mount's neck.

He'd gathered a small pile of branches, squatted and lit a fire, his back to her while he worked the embers. Flames flickered and flared, bathing the camp with a gossamer glow.

Callie Mae had never been a coward, but she was reluctant to step from around her horse just yet. TJ could hardly see her here, deep in the shadows. Given his dark mood, he might not appreciate her staring.

But she couldn't help it.

Her gaze dallied over his shoulders and the way his shirt stretched over their breadth when he moved. His torso tapered to a lean waist; the denim of his Levi's pulled taut across the corded muscle of his thighs and the curve of his buttocks.

Her veins stirred with awareness all over again.

TJ Grier was pure cowboy. Pure male. Strong and capable and driven.

As much as she hated to admit it, Callie Mae had always known that about him. He would never have earned her parents' respect and that of the entire C Bar C outfit if he wasn't those things—and more.

Unexpectedly, something elusive and unsettling stirred inside Callie Mae.

A softening.

She had to stop it before it got worse.

Thinking about TJ as anything more than being responsible for Danny's death was foolish, and her staring was only a product of their circumstances. He'd put a gun to her head, for pity's sake. Forced her to be alone with him. What else could she do but keep an eye on him?

Callie Mae dragged her gaze away, began untying her bedroll from behind the saddle and put Kullen in her thoughts instead.

Dear, handsome Kullen.

Thinking of him gave her comfort. Reminded her

how well-groomed he always looked with his hair combed and shined with tonic. How delicious he smelled with expensive cologne smoothed on his skin. He had impeccable taste in his clothing, his suits a perfect fit. Charming and intelligent, often amusing and insightful, Kullen was as far from a cowboy as one could be.

Which was why she loved him, she reminded herself firmly. He was different than the other men she'd known while growing up on the C Bar C. Refined and worldly.

Boot steps crunched the dirt, and her thoughts jumped right back to TJ. He approached his horse and busied himself untying his bedroll, too. Ignoring her. As if he didn't care if she stayed or left.

Her lips thinned. He acted as if she'd offended him with her warning not to hurt her. What did he think she should do? Trust him? After what had happened with Danny?

Yet, a tiny voice insisted if he intended to hurt her, he would've done so by now. God knew he'd had plenty of opportunity while they'd ridden together tonight, both of them alone on the Texas range these past hours.

She pulled off the bedroll and threw it over her shoulder.

Maybe she'd been wrong to accuse him.

"Set it over by the fire," TJ ordered, dropping his own bedroll to the ground while he took off the saddlebags.

The gruffness in his voice did little to soothe her mood, but she knew better than to argue. After doing what he instructed, she headed back toward her horse and busied herself unbuckling the cinch.

She took a breath, then let it out again.

"I'm sorry," she said.

Carrying the saddlebags in one hand, the bedroll in the other, he turned, headed toward the fire, added his gear to hers.

"For what?" he asked, coming back.

"You know very well 'for what.'"

"Remind me."

Damn him. "For saying you'd hurt me and for thinking you might."

He grunted, bent over the cinch on his own saddle. "What changed your mind?"

The strap on hers dangled; she reached up to grasp the cantle and horn, a hand on each, and paused. "I suppose it's from having known you for so long. It's not something you—" she hesitated, searching for the right words "—you would've done. Before Danny died, at least."

"Not after, either."

Rising up on tiptoe, she tightened her grip and pulled off the saddle. "Time will tell, won't it?"

He scowled. "I've known you since you were a scrawny kid in pigtails, Callie Mae. I've watched you grow up into a beautiful woman." He tugged the saddle from his horse, too. "The C Bar C is the only home I've ever known. I don't even want to think what kind of life I would've had if Carina hadn't taken me in."

In that, Callie Mae believed him. Maggie hadn't

latched on to mothering like most women did. She'd never been strong enough for it. TJ had been left to fend for himself at an early age, but he'd thrived at the ranch, among the C Bar C outfit, and his skill with horses had grown year after year.

"So why would I throw away a damned good life by hurting the only real family I've ever known?" he demanded. "Maggie excepted."

"Do you think I haven't asked myself that very thing, oh, a million times or so?"

"Well, you can stop asking yourself, Callie Mae," he shot back. "Because I wouldn't."

An unexpected welling of tears had her whirling away from him. If he didn't sound so sincere, so blamably determined to make her believe him...

She didn't want her hate for him to slip. She didn't want to feel this ridiculous *doubt.*

TJ was guilty of killing Danny. He'd admitted as much in front of the judge, so why should he stand here and expect her to believe anything but that?

God, she missed Kullen. When she was with him, she never had doubts about TJ. Not like this.

"In case you have any crazy ideas about running back to your precious intended the minute my back is turned," TJ said with appalling perception, his voice low with warning. "Don't." He dropped his saddle next to the pile of bedrolls. "You're liable to get lost out there. And the range is full of the wild."

"It'd serve you right if I did run back to him." Callie Mae knew she sounded petulant, but there was no help for it. It was how she felt about this predicament she found herself in, being with TJ and all confused. "But I'm not stupid."

"I've never known you to be, so don't start now."

She dropped her saddle next to his and gave full concentration to readying her bedroll for the night. She shook out the blanket, laid it over the patch of grass nearest the fire, then smoothed it on top, hoping if she pretended he wasn't there, he'd go away.

He didn't.

"Have you slept with him, Callie Mae?" he demanded.

Her gaze darted to him on a small gasp. "Kullen?"

"And don't tell me it's none of my business, because I'm making it mine."

She stood, faced him square. Firelight flickered across the strong angles of his face. The hard line of his mouth. He held her gaze with his own, intense beneath the Stetson's brim.

The tentacles of a lie formed on her tongue. It'd serve him right if she told him she'd shared a bed with Kullen before their marriage. She could make up all sorts of lurid details and throw them in his face. Retribution for his audacity in asking such a personal question.

But she didn't.

She was a Lockett, after all. She refused to stoop so low.

"Think what you want about me marrying Kullen, TJ, but the answer to your question is no. I've never slept with him or anyone else, for that matter."

The barest hint of a smile softened his hard mouth.

"Good," he said. "Very good."

He poked his bedroll, then, with the toe of his boot. The thing began to unfurl, little by little, until it stretched out straight, right next to hers.

Seeing those blankets laying so close together, Callie Mae's mouth went dry.

"Well, then, Miss Lockett," he drawled. "Looks like I get to be the first."

Chapter Eight

~~~~~~~~~

"Will I walk again?"

Kullen's voice shook from dread as he pinned his gaze on the white-haired surgeon bent over him.

"I removed the bullet, but it hit the bone and scattered fragments. I cleaned the surrounding muscle as best I could." Doctor Feldman lifted Kullen's sleeve and injected the morphine that would stave off pain so fiery that Kullen was tempted to chop off his leg to be free from it. "However, the chances for blood poisoning are high."

Kullen's flesh turned clammy. The man avoided looking at him—and had yet to answer his question.

"But will I *walk?*" he demanded.

"With help." Feldman removed the needle, pressed a piece of cotton against the skin to blot a drop of blood. "I hope."

Kullen swallowed. "What kind of help?"

"Until the leg has a chance to heal, I'm afraid you'll be on a long period of bed rest. Then, once you're strong enough, a wheelchair will be necessary. Perhaps you'll use a cane, eventually, if you're able."

Kullen's heart pounded in horror.

A wheelchair? A cane, *if he was able?*

"The leg will always be weak," Feldman continued, straightening. "Unfortunately, you won't walk unassisted in some way—" he hesitated "—for the rest of your life."

The news was worse than Kullen feared. Nausea roiled in his stomach. Rage. TJ Grier had cold-bloodedly maimed him, and if Kullen could, he'd heave himself out of his hospital bed, hunt TJ down and put him through the same kind of misery. Or maybe he'd just shoot TJ dead where he stood—

"Right now, rest is the best thing for you, Mr. Brosius." The surgeon gave him a medicinal smile. "I'll be by in the morning to check on you."

He patted Kullen's shoulder and left.

Kullen gaped at the closed door. Wasn't there something else Feldman could do? Another kind of surgery to make him whole again?

His head fell back against the pillow. God, he didn't deserve this. Not when he was so close. So damned close to marrying Callie Mae.

Despair rolled through him. A cattlewoman like her, heiress to the almighty C Bar C ranch, she could have any man she wanted.

She wouldn't want a cripple who couldn't walk across the room by himself.

Kullen's breathing quickened. He could get sick, too. Like Feldman warned.

The chances for blood poisoning are high...

He might die.

The despair intensified, the certainty he'd all but lost his chance to get his hands on the C Bar C and that pile of beautiful money Callie Mae stood to inherit.

But the worst, the absolute worst, was being deprived of a prime opportunity for revenge against her stepfather.

He closed his eyes and groaned. Fell backward in time to how Penn McClure left him orphaned and penniless a decade ago.

As the son of Bill Brockway, a master counterfeiter, Kullen had been given a taste of the riches that illicit boodle could bring. Until McClure, then a government agent, found his father and killed him in the hallway of Denver's Brown Palace Hotel.

Not even the drug numbing Kullen's mind could help him forget his struggles to survive afterward. His vow to get even.

Callie Mae had given him the perfect opportunity, thanks to her grandmother, Mavis. The old biddy never suspected that he intended to use her precious granddaughter for his revenge. Even better, Callie Mae never did, either. The spoiled bitch was too busy living her life of comfort to ever guess his intentions.

Kullen gritted his teeth. He'd worked hard at getting this far with his plan. Years' worth of hard work. He'd changed his name to Brosius. Plotted and schemed. Spent half of his life waiting to triumph.

And now TJ Grier had ruined it for him.

"Kullen. You doing all right?"

Kullen dragged himself out of the past and opened his eyes. His cousin, Emmett Ralston, stood beside his bed. He still wore his faded blue shirt and dirty denims from earlier in the day when he played groomer for TJ at Preston Farm.

Kullen hadn't heard him come in. He strained to focus on the bearded face.

"Does it look like I'm all right?" he muttered, tried to sit up and failed. He cursed his pain, his weakness. "Where have you been?"

"Following Grier and the Lockett woman, but I lost them in the dark." Emmett's hooded gaze took him in. "Did the jockey and Grier's mother bring you here?"

"Yes." Kullen had been forced to lie in the back of the wagon like a helpless sack of potatoes, and the ride to Amarillo had been agony. "Took forever to get to this damned hospital."

"How bad's your leg?" Emmett asked, frowning.

"Bad."

"What're you going to do?"

"Not much I can do but lay here, is there?" he snapped.

Kullen closed his eyes again. He had to find a way to track down Callie Mae and convince her he could still be the husband she'd always believed he would be. He had to salvage his dream for revenge before it was too late.

"He knows something," Emmett said.

Kullen's thinking wavered, and he opened his eyes again. "Who?"

"Grier."

He fought to comprehend. "How do you know he does?"

"He claimed it, back at Boomer's."

Kullen tried to remember and failed. He blamed the morphine, the way the drug turned his brain soft.

"What did he say?" The demand sounded slurred, but he couldn't help it.

Emmett kept watching him. "He said you were responsible for killin' McClure's kid. That the way you were acting proved it."

Kullen replayed the scene in his mind and couldn't think of what he'd done to make TJ know he was responsible for anything. Except being determined to take Blue from him. "He can't prove a thing."

"No," Emmett said.

"You were careful, weren't you?"

"I told you I was."

Sleep beckoned. The bliss of peace. Freedom from pain. The worries of revenge and fears of failure.

"Tell me what you want me to do," Emmett said quietly.

Kullen took comfort in his cousin's loyalty. They were like brothers, the two of them. They needed each other to survive. To triumph. Emmett would do whatever Kullen told him. He always had. That's how it was between them.

Kullen gave the orders. Emmett obeyed them.

And time was running out.

"Find TJ and kill him," he whispered. "Then bring Callie Mae to me."

* * *

TJ woke the next morning knowing he had to tell her what he'd done.

He stacked his hands beneath his head and stared up into the inky sky. Dawn had yet to dribble hues of pink and orange along the horizon, but it would soon. By then, TJ intended to be up and ready to ride.

Which meant if he wanted to talk, he had to do it now.

He'd spent most of the night debating the wisdom of telling Callie Mae what little he knew. His secret had been secret for so long, it downright scared him to bring everything out into the open with her.

He had no idea how she'd handle what he had to say, but she deserved to know. Might be she'd quit fighting him on his need to find Blue. Maybe quit hating him so much, too. Regardless, TJ hoped to convince her she couldn't marry Kullen Brosius. By the time things were said and done, she'd know TJ would fight to keep her from it.

His head swiveled toward the dark shape of her body beside him, and the blood in his groin stirred. She'd been restless during the night. Tossed and turned. He figured she had just about as much on her mind as he did on his, and the need to hold her, to take away this damned barrier that had come between them—

She'd learn there were some benefits to sharing her bedroll with a man. With him. Pleasures beyond warmth, safety. She'd come to know she could trust him, that he was nothing like the man she believed he was—an unfair picture colored by Kullen and a crooked judge who left more questions than there seemed answers for.

Anger stirred inside TJ yet again from how Kullen conspired against him and cost TJ everything he'd ever known. But he fought the anger down. God knew, he'd experienced enough fury these past months already, and what had that got him but a full load of frustration?

He focused on Callie Mae instead and the explanation he intended to give her. He shifted to his side, raised himself up on one elbow. Already, the night had begun to lift, and he could see her better.

She laid with her back to him, her blanket pulled up to her shoulder. Her braid trailed behind her, loose and haphazard, and dark strands of cinnamon-shaded hair rested against her cheek.

There went that warming in his groin again. A growing lust. He relished the privilege of being with her. Soaking in the sight of her. All he had to do was lower his head to smell her skin, to nuzzle her neck and feel her warmth. What would it be like to wake up next to her every dawn?

"I know what you're thinking, TJ Grier, but if you so much as touch me, I'll make sure you never have need of a woman again."

The fervent warning startled him. Amused him, too, that she read him so easily, and he hadn't even known she was awake.

His mouth curved. "Guess if you're knowing what I'm thinking, it means you're laying there thinking the same thing."

He reached toward her to brush away the curls from her face so he could see her better, but her blanket lowered, and Kullen's Colt derringer appeared, aimed right at the heart of TJ's lust.

Which cooled in a hurry.

"I think I'm thinking something different," she said smoothly.

He'd yet to touch her. Carefully, he drew back. "What the *hell* are you doing, Callie Mae?"

"Trying to keep you from adding rape to your crimes, that's all."

His patience snapped, and in one sharp movement, he snatched the gun from her grasp. She squeaked and grabbed for it again, but he tossed it into the grass, out of her reach.

Insulted beyond words, he sat up and leveled her with a scathing glance.

"You're a beautiful woman, Callie Mae, and I'll not deny I've got a healthy appreciation for it, but you can be *damned* sure if anything should happen between us, you'll be a happy and willing participant."

She sat up, too. Sniffed and tossed her head, like a haughty filly. "Nothing will ever happen between us, TJ. I'm almost a married woman, in case you've forgotten. I'm going to save myself for Kullen."

"And isn't that a shame?"

"Not for him it isn't."

TJ eyed her sitting there, looking dignified and righteous and every bit her mother's daughter. Kullen didn't deserve her fidelity, however well-meaning she meant it, and how could the fool have kept from bedding her? Branding her as forever his?

Admirable restraint? Virtuous honor?

Or was he in love with her money more?

TJ's lip curled. "Does he ever lust for you, Callie Mae?"

"What?" She appeared taken aback. "I don't—that's none of your business. Why would you ask such a thing?"

"Tell me he can't keep his hands off you. Convince me that you're on his mind every minute of every day."

"I'm not going to try to convince you of anything. He's a perfect gentleman, TJ, and I don't want to continue this conversation with you." She tossed aside the blanket and would've bolted to her feet if TJ hadn't grabbed her wrist first and kept her sitting. Firmly. While trying not to be aware of how slender her bones were against his fingers.

"You can't convince me because he doesn't want you," he grated. "He wants your money and your ranch. He wants the Lockett in you, Callie Mae. Nothing else."

"Let go of me." She yanked.

"When this is all said and done, you'll believe me. You'll *see* it."

"I refuse to stay with you any longer and listen to your constant demeaning of the man I intend to marry. Find your horse by yourself. Kullen needs me."

"He needs you, all right. But not like you think."

Her nostrils flared. She clamped her mouth shut.

End of argument.

TJ released her in frustration.

This stubbornness of hers, it was making him crazy.

He reached for his boots, thumped them upside down in case anything had crawled in during the night, and glared at the derringer lying in the grass. That she felt a need to steal it from his saddlebag and keep it with her rankled all over again.

He pulled on one boot and caught her sullen expression. He pulled on the second and wondered if anything he'd said had gotten through to her.

"I need some coffee," she muttered.

TJ could relate. Some of his frustration eased. "I'll make some."

Far as he knew, she'd never made the brew over a campfire. Sourdough, head cook for the C Bar C outfit, was responsible for the job, but TJ could make a fair pot when he had to.

The corners of Callie Mae's mouth dipped. "Sleeping on the ground might be easy for you, but I was never made for it."

Knowing that, too, he grunted. Callie Mae tended to favor the softer side of life, a difference between her and her mother. Carina had been born tougher, could hold her own on just about anything involving the harshest aspects of the C Bar C, no matter the circumstances.

But that's what fascinated TJ about Callie Mae. Her softness. Her being purely female.

"You'll feel better once you start moving." He stood, bringing Kullen's gun with him for safekeeping.

He sensed her watching him while he stoked the fire

to boil water, then went for the coffeepot and cups that Stinky Dale sent along. She sat with her knees pulled up to her chest, as if determined to keep her distance from him, making him worry she might make good on her threat to leave him and return to Kullen.

"Why does having this horse—Blue—mean so much to you, TJ?" she asked.

He didn't expect her to try to understand. Why would she, when she'd been handed her legacy on the proverbial silver spoon? By the time she'd grown up to appreciate it, her parents had already sweated years into building a heritage she could be proud of.

"I've always admired a fine horse," he said. "Blue's finer than most."

She shook her head, telling him she realized he avoided her question. "There are lots of fine horses in this country. In fact, I could buy you a new one, TJ. Another fine horse to replace Blue."

TJ narrowed his eyes over her. "You think it's as easy as all that?"

"Tell me why it isn't."

He found a small tin of Arbuckles, opened it, then remembered he still needed water to fill the pot.

"Why Blue?" she persisted. "And don't tell me it's because you want to race him. There are plenty of 'fine' racehorses in this country, too."

He gave up on making the coffee but remained hunkered next to the campfire. He rested a forearm on his thigh and locked his gaze on her.

"Because everything I have is in that horse, Callie

Mae. I bought him with my last dime. I have nothing left, thanks to that lowlife you plan to marry, but Blue is the one thing I can call mine."

Tiny furrows formed between her brows, showing she wanted to understand. She'd gotten him off-track in his intent to confess his part in Danny's death, but her need to know Blue's place in it was important, too.

"I've never seen a horse with as much spirit." TJ's thoughts turned back to the first time he'd laid eyes on the stallion. The decision to travel to Kentucky had been a difficult one, the risks of his plan high. But one look at the sleek, graceful then-two-year-old, and TJ had fallen in love. "He was born to run. He can win any race I put him in."

"You want him for the money he can make you," she said.

He ignored her bite of sarcasm. "That's only part of it."

"Kullen said Blue is signed up to race in Fort Worth."

"Yes." Information gleaned from Emmett Ralston, a conspiracy that still set TJ's teeth on edge.

"For a lucrative purse?"

"Respectable." TJ endured her interrogation even as he wondered just what she was leading up to. "Winning Fort Worth won't make me rich, but it'd be a start."

"Precisely my point."

Callie Mae pulled on her boots and rose to her feet with an impatience that had TJ feeling some of the same.

"Which is?" he demanded, rising, too.

"That you have some sort of—of ridiculous notion that racing is going to be your salvation."

He went still, replayed the conversation in his mind, tried to figure what he said that made her think such a thing.

"You're wrong," he said, failing. "It's not."

"Excuse me." Briskly, she strode toward him, and the pot still lying at his feet. "I have a strong need for a cup of coffee, which is not going to get made while we stand here and have this useless conversation on the virtues of an abominable sport."

Useless?

An abominable sport?

Wasn't she listening to anything he'd said?

His jaw hardened, and he kicked the pot aside before she could grab it. He grasped her shoulders and forced her to stand in front of him. Her head tilted back, and her stormy gaze clashed with his.

"A man can have plenty in this world, or he can have little, but if he doesn't have his good name, then he has nothing. You hear me? Nothing." He loosened his grip. She didn't move away, and he took heart from it. "That's what happened when Danny died, Callie Mae. I lost my good name and a whole lot more, besides. And if you'd just let go of that damn Lockett pride of yours, you'd know I'd never have wanted to hurt him."

The depths of her eyes turned brooding. Troubled. "I don't think you know how badly I want to believe you wouldn't." She stepped back and squared her shoulders, as if she'd revealed too much. "But it's too late. You already have. You've hurt all of us."

TJ clenched his fists to keep from taking her into his arms and showing her how much he regretted the pain he'd caused.

"Which is why I need to find Blue. To find the truth, Callie Mae," he said. "To help me prove I'm not the man Kullen made me to be. And I want you with me when I do."

She turned away, toward the horizon, now bold with pink and orange and gold. The line of her shoulders softened, as if she wearied of the battle she fought. The responsibility she carried. Her need to believe.

"It could take days to find him, TJ," she said quietly. "He could be anywhere out there."

"You don't think that scares me?"

A sound rumbled, then. In the distance. His head lifted in search of it. Callie Mae's did, too, and they both swung toward the intrusion.

A cloud took shape in the haze of the valley. Dust raised by hordes of pounding hooves. Horses. An entire manada.

And leading them all was Blue.

Chapter Nine

Callie Mae had seen Blue Whistler for only a few moments at Boomer Preston's, but even in the chaos that ensued, she would never forget the horse's magnificence.

She saw it again now.

His long mane flying, the stallion led the others like a king led his subjects, and she stood riveted from the sight of his grace. His speed. His mastery over the herd of mustangs.

They raced through the mesquite-covered valley in wild and breathtaking abandon, as if they ran for the pure joy of it. Their hooves threw back clods of dirt and churning dust. The valley rocked with their power and speed.

But TJ only cursed and shoved Callie Mae toward their mounts, tethered at the edge of the camp.

"We have to go after 'em," he shouted. "Hurry!"

The urgency in his command shot adrenaline through her veins, and she bolted toward the horses.

TJ was already there, grabbing saddle blankets from the ground, throwing one on the buckskin, the other at her. The roan pranced, ears pricked, nickering low in his throat. She had all she could do to get the saddle on and cinched tight.

TJ vaulted onto the buckskin's back.

"Stay with me," he ordered. His horse pulled at the bit, eager to give chase. "Y'hear? Don't fall back."

"I won't." She pushed her feet into the stirrups, grabbed for the reins and settled in her seat.

He didn't have to tell her twice. An untamed horse could turn violent at any threat, and TJ would be a formidable one. The whole bunch could turn lawless.

Apprehensive at what lay ahead—this precarious opportunity to get Blue back—she tore after TJ. She had no time to think of the danger. Of failure or of all that could go wrong. She knew only that she had to help. That suddenly, it became unthinkable to refuse.

His shirt billowing from the chase, TJ rode low over the buckskin's neck and slapped the reins again and again. The staccato of hooves hammered the earth and filled Callie Mae's ears. Wind rushed across her face, pulled at her hair. The land rose, dipped, stretched, and still the mustangs raced, with Blue gallantly at their head.

They approached a low ridge, and finally, TJ slowed. He held up a hand for her to do the same, and she drew up to a halt next to him.

"Looks like they needed water," he said, breathing hard.

The manada mingled in a meadow a short distance

away from a stream, a runoff from a fork of the Red River. She counted twenty-two horses, a misfit band of assorted colors and breeds and ages. Mares, most of them accompanied by their foals.

"So why aren't they drinking?" she asked.

"They're waiting for their leader to test the water first. See him over there?"

TJ pointed toward a pinto stallion, standing off by himself on a small hill. His stance appeared fierce, protective. Dominant.

"The master," TJ said.

Fascinated, Callie Mae stared. Dirty white with dark patches over his face, neck and chest, the pinto had nothing about him to warrant his position in the herd except for arrogance, a power that kept the rest of the horses humble and waiting.

But Blue Whistler didn't seem to notice. Or much care.

The midnight-black hide gleamed with sweat beneath the morning sun. Long-legged, his body contoured with muscle, he fed on the gramma grass at his leisure, oblivious to his presence among mongrels— the mares hovering curious around him. Around his sleek neck, he still wore the lead rope from Boomer's. The length had been bitten off, and it proved a stark reminder of how TJ had lost him.

Regret swirled through Callie Mae from her part in it. TJ would still have his prized horse and neither of them would be out here giving chase, if she hadn't burst into his life and demanded he give her Tres Pinos Valley.

But Kullen was to blame, too. She forced herself to acknowledge it. He'd whipped out his derringer, a weapon she didn't even know he carried, and ordered TJ's jockey, Lodi, to hand the racehorse over to Preston Farm's shifty-eyed groomer.

Emmett Ralston.

Why? They seemed such an unlikely pair. What could their connection be?

Her troubled glance moved to TJ, studying the manada with his jaw set hard. In his haste to chase after Blue, he'd neglected to grab his Stetson, and sunlight glinted his wind-tossed hair tawny gold. A lock fell over his forehead; more fell over the collar of his shirt. But it was the dark bristle roughening his cheeks that gave him the look of an outlaw, rugged and dangerous and exciting...

Her blood warmed, deep inside. So deep, it left her shaken. That she could think of him as anything but the man responsible for her young brother's death was unforgivable.

Even though that's what she was doing. Thinking of him in ways she shouldn't.

Thinking which should be of Kullen instead.

But wasn't.

Never like this.

"I don't like the way he's watching Blue," TJ said, grim.

His low voice chased away her meddlesome thoughts, and she drew in a slow breath, refocused them on the master stallion.

"Why?" she asked.

"He's jealous."

Callie Mae could see it, too. How the pinto appeared tense, unmoving. Biding his time, like a snake in the grass. "He *should* be jealous. A ruffian like him doesn't have a thing on Blue."

"The stallion is smart, and he's strong. That's why he's the leader. He'll fight dirty to guard the mares and keep them in his band." TJ squinted an eye, swept a slow glance over the range. "Once he notices us watching him, he'll feel threatened and run. We might never catch the manada then."

"What about Blue?" Callie Mae began to feel her own worry build. "Will he run with them if he sees you?"

TJ's mouth quirked. "I'd like to think he's been missing me, right along with square meals and a clean stall back at Boomer's. Truth is, he's gotten a taste of freedom. A horse with as much spirit as he has—"

He halted. Callie Mae finished what he didn't say. "Could turn wild, too."

"Afraid so."

And all the training TJ had given him, all he'd worked for, the time and money spent, the dreams he'd made to rebuild his life after Danny's killing…would be lost.

Once, Callie Mae would've gloated over his misfortune. She would've felt he deserved everything he got.

But now?

She didn't. At least, not so much.

Blue moseyed over to the water's edge. He couldn't know the worry TJ felt over him, she mused.

He'd be oblivious to the trouble he made to those who loved him most.

Suddenly, the pinto screamed and leapt off the hill toward him. Several mares whinnied; foals scattered. TJ breathed a fervent curse.

Blue, clearly startled, jumped back to face his aggressor, and it appeared the two—one territorial, the other untrained to the ways of the wild—would do battle.

Both reared and flailed their hooves, but Blue backed off first, and the confrontation ended. The master stallion cantered back to the hill, apparently confident his place as leader remained unquestioned.

"That was only a warning," TJ grated. "Next time, he won't let Blue off so lightly."

"No," she murmured, knowing it.

"Blue was never born to fight." He reached for a coil of rope, tied to his saddle. "I have to get him out of there."

After seeing the pinto's outburst, the risks seemed worse than ever. The horse looked mean enough to have already reserved himself a place in hell.

"Just tell me what I should do," she said.

"Stay here. That's what you should do."

She blinked at him. "Why?"

"It's too dangerous."

"For me, but not for you?" Exasperation snapped through her demand.

"I can't let you get involved. All those horses—if you get thrown or if they come at you and knock you out of your seat, you'll be trampled into sausage."

"It won't happen. I'll make sure it won't."

"It could, Callie Mae. Faster than you'd know."

She resisted the validity of his logic, straightened in the saddle and gathered the reins. "We can fret about it, or we can ride down and get your horse back. But you'll not sit there and tell me to do nothing."

He didn't move.

"I'd never forgive myself if you got hurt," he said, his tone rough.

"I don't suppose I'd like it much, either."

"You don't have to do this."

Keenly aware of the seconds rolling by, she considered the manada. The dirty-looking pinto in particular. The fierce picture he made. Domineering and proud.

TJ was an expert rider. He lived and breathed horseflesh. He always had, always would.

But in the eyes of the mustangs' leader, TJ was an enemy. A threat to freedom and all that was his. To protect what was his, he'd wage a vicious battle.

Why should TJ fight him alone?

TJ's worry moved her, in spite of everything. She reached out and touched his forearm.

"I want to," she said.

The tendons in his arm tightened, and his hand covered hers. A work-roughened hand, strong and warm. Incredibly gentle.

"I'd be crazy to let you…"

His voice trailed off, and he slipped his fingers beneath her palm, lifted her hand and pressed a kiss to her knuckles.

Callie Mae stilled. The simplest of gestures, expressed in humility, in concern—he'd taken the time to show her, as if he could do nothing less, and it was nearly her undoing.

She pulled her hand away. He couldn't affect her like this. Make her all soft and unsettled inside. Too much stood between them. Too much always would.

"He knows we're here." She swung her head, her tone matter-of-fact. A trifle unsteady. "The master stallion."

TJ nodded. "I know. He still hasn't taken a drink."

She understood the mustang leader now. The life he lived. That he'd never have anything less than pure freedom.

"He's biding his time." She noted how he stood on the hill, his stance alert. Not even a hair on his tail twitched. "He's waiting for us to make the first move."

"Yes." TJ studied the rest of the band. "As soon as we do, he'll start the manada running. The mustangs will follow the lead mare, and he's going to run like the devil with them."

Callie Mae nodded. "Which one is the lead mare?"

"The dun, with the dark stripe down her back. Standing closest to Blue."

Callie Mae found her. A thick-haired broomtail with a large head and long ears. "I see her."

"Blue will be leading. There's a box canyon ahead. I'll turn him into it. And you—" he hesitated, as if he still warred with his worry she'd be hurt "—you make sure the mare keeps on running."

"Should be easy enough." For the second time that morning, adrenaline curled through her.

"At the first sign of trouble, back off. Y'hear me, Callie Mae? I'll come around for you."

She'd been riding a long time—since she was old enough to sit a horse. She could do this. "I'm no fool, TJ."

"Let's hope not." He loosened the slipknot on his rope and made a loop big enough to throw over Blue's head, then switched the coiled lariat to his left hand. "Are you ready?"

"Just waiting on you," she retorted.

His gaze lingered over her for a brief moment. Then, amazingly, he waggled his brows in reckless anticipation—which another time, another place— would've been amusing, if he wasn't so deliberately snubbing the danger that lay ahead.

And there her blood went, warming with excitement again. An awareness of him she shouldn't be feeling.

Then, his focus changed and sharpened over the manada. He kicked his heels into the buckskin's ribs, giving the horse his head in a hard gallop down the ridge.

Callie Mae drew in a breath and followed.

Riding hard, the thunder of hooves resonated around her. Dust coated her lips, her throat. Ahead, TJ's swift approach startled the mares, and they bolted away from the stream. Their shrieks filled the air. Foals scattered wildly, crying for their mothers.

In the confusion, Callie Mae lost sight of the lead mare, and she raked a frantic gaze over the ragtag band, their thick hides dirty, tails and manes tangled with cockleburs. This close to the herd, their numbers seemed to double; their size and speed, too.

She couldn't find Blue. Or the master stallion. For a moment, she floundered, needing direction. The roan veered and dodged fleeing horses; Callie Mae squeezed her thighs against his sides to keep herself in the saddle.

Then, as if by a miracle, the herd took shape and fell into a formation they alone knew. The pinto circled behind to force the slower horses to keep up, then ran alongside on the far left, adding his impetus to the mare's to hasten their flight.

Hunched over the buckskin's neck, riding fast, TJ inched past the lead mare. Closer toward Blue. Callie Mae stayed behind him, keeping him in sight as he gained ground on the black thoroughbred.

"Hee-yah! Hee-yah!"

At TJ's persistent yells, Blue made a sudden, panicked swerve toward the right; the box canyon TJ had known was there. He swung the lariat; the loop spun and dropped over Blue's neck. The hemp jerked tight, and the thoroughbred's gait faltered. TJ moved up beside him at full gallop, close, so close an arrow of fear shot through Callie Mae at what he would do.

That he intended to abandon his mount in midstride pushed her heart right into her throat. He was going to leap right onto Blue…oh, God, if either horse veered unexpectedly, TJ could fall beneath those hammering hooves…

But he vaulted onto Blue's back with more ease, more agility, more *daring* than any man should possess, and swiftly wrapped the rope around the long black nose. Head swinging at the loss of his freedom, Blue trotted into the canyon with no way to escape.

TJ had regained his stake on his prized horse, and Callie Mae was all but shaking from it. Riding neck and neck with the lead mare, she left TJ behind, her concentration forced on keeping the rest of the herd moving.

Looking wild-eyed and scared, the shabby-haired dun ran as if her tail was on fire. Most likely, she'd never been in such close proximity to a human being before, and Callie Mae took pity on her. This far from Blue and TJ, the mare wouldn't be much of a threat anyway. Not anymore.

"Go on!" If Callie Mae had her hat, she would've waved it to make her point. "Get out of here! Go!"

She fell back, and the manada thundered onward, wrapped in a cloying veil of dust, into the horizon.

Callie Mae tucked wind-blown strands of hair behind her ear and heaved the tension off her chest. Thank God they were gone.

She turned the roan around and spied TJ's horse wandering up ahead, reins dragging. At her approach, the buckskin nickered, and she crooned softly to calm him, then bent from the saddle to take the leathers. Tired and docile, he followed her at an easy canter toward the canyon.

But the shrill sounds of screaming horses threw her pulse into pounding alarm again. She kicked her mount into a run toward the opening and spied Blue on his hind legs, engaged in battle with the fierce pinto. Their angry shrieks echoed throughout the canyon.

The stallions struck each other with their hooves. Bit with their sharp teeth. Lunged and swerved and twisted.

Only sheer strength could've kept TJ on Blue's back as he fought to keep them both from the attack. Callie Mae knew he couldn't hang on long, not without a saddle and with those powerful bodies thrashing in combat. His yells to scare off the pinto were ineffective; the manada leader was determined to remind Blue who was boss in this part of the range and that TJ was a threat to all he claimed.

Any moment, TJ could lose his grip and be thrown. One stomp of those heavy hooves would break bones, crush his insides—

She rode faster. "Hee-yah! Hee-yah!"

Blue jerked in distraction from her yells, but the pinto seemed unaffected by them. He reared, filled the air with long, shrill whinnies. He slammed his bulk into the thoroughbred, and Blue stumbled sideways. TJ grappled to keep his seat. The pinto charged again, and TJ went down on the hard ground and rolled.

"Hee-yah! Hee-yah!"

Callie Mae kept riding. She was almost there, only seconds away. Time she needed to keep the horses moving, away from TJ. The stallion might think TJ was his enemy, but in a moment, he'd know she was, too. She had the advantage. She had speed. She had her horse and TJ's, two forces against one, and if the stallion valued his freedom, he'd realize he'd be cornered in the canyon if he didn't turn and high-tail it out in a hurry.

His taste for the fight clearly gone, Blue retreated deeper into the safety of the gorge. The pinto didn't follow, but swung toward Callie Mae.

His eyes turned sharp, assessing. His stance changed, readied for flight. He tossed a high-handed glance at Blue, as if to flaunt his triumph, his superiority at being the master of mustangs, and just before Callie Mae reached him, he leapt into a full run and fled in the direction of his manada.

Chapter Ten

～～～～～～

TJ needed a minute for the stars to clear.

It'd been a good long while since he'd been thrown from a horse, and landing on the hard canyon dirt had rattled every bone in his body. Pain shot through his brain, telling him his head took part of the fall. He tasted dust, smelled it, lay facedown with his cheek pressed into it.

But he could breathe, and he could think. Some. Better now that the stars began to thin. Shrill neighing penetrated his consciousness, and he strained to remember where he was. And why.

A woman's shout distracted the remembering. His eyelids cracked open; he strained to focus on her, on the blur moving not far in front of him.

The blur cleared, and an oath choked out of his throat.

Callie Mae and that damned mustang stallion.

Blue.

TJ spied his horse farther away, deeper in the

canyon. The need to go to him, make sure he wasn't injured, that he wouldn't run again gripped TJ, and he planted his hands shoulder-high and tried to push himself up, but his muscles locked. He sank back down on a groan.

The neighing ended. Hooves pounded the canyon floor. Then footsteps, Callie Mae running toward him.

"TJ. Oh, God, TJ!"

She sounded frantic, scared, and words to assure her he was all right failed him. He wasn't sure he was just yet. He only needed a little more time to find out, to get his strength back. A few more seconds...

But the way she threw herself on her knees and started running her hands over his back and arms got him to feeling again in a hurry.

"TJ, are you all right? Oh, here, roll over." She yanked on his shirt, used it for leverage to pull him onto his side. "Let me look at you."

He let her worry over him. When had she ever? The high-and-mighty Callie Mae Lockett, fussing about him, a lowly cowboy in her mother's outfit—

She tugged him onto his back, and thankfully, when she did, nothing hurt.

"Look at me, TJ," she pleaded. "Say something."

Her cool fingers tapped repeatedly at his cheeks to pull him out of the darkness. She didn't know he was already out, that he *liked* her fussing, the touching part being the best. He kept his eyes closed so she'd keep on touching him.

"I don't see any blood," she muttered, and he

imagined her checking him over but good. Her hands poked and prodded over his shoulders and chest. "I can't tell if anything's broken, TJ. Please wake up so you can help me!"

Didn't seem right to keep on deceiving her, not when she sounded genuinely upset. Far as he knew, there wasn't much wrong with him, but her thinking there might and being on the verge of tears over it filled him with a boldness he'd kept in check too damn long.

Emitting a mock growl, he hooked his arm around her waist and pulled her down to roll with him, flipping their positions in one quick motion. She cried out in surprise, landed flat on her back and stared up at him with wide, startled eyes.

"TJ!" she exclaimed, breathless.

He took full advantage of her prone position to keep her pinned beneath him with the weight of his body. Fate had blessed him with an opportunity he'd probably never have again. Callie Mae had been part of his dreams for so long, he couldn't remember a time when she wasn't.

And having her like this was one hell of a dream come true, and his groin lit into a slow fire.

"TJ! What do you think you're—are you *hurt?*"

"If I was, reckon I'm not anymore." His mouth curved in amusement. Feeling her slim thighs against his, her hips and belly, too, well, he'd all but forgotten the knock his head had taken.

Her eyes narrowed. "You were playing possum with me."

He managed an innocent look. "No, I wasn't."

"Well, you scared me!" Her hand fisted, and she smacked his shoulder. "What were you thinking, jumping onto Blue at full gallop back there?"

Is that what she was upset about? His amusement faded. "I couldn't let him get away, could I?"

"So you just hopped on him, as if you were born without a lick of sense. Never mind the two dozen mustangs running wild alongside that could have tromped all over you if you fell off." She glared up at him, her eyes spitting blue lightning. "Would've served you right if you did. Get tromped."

His smile found its way back. Her vexation charmed him. "I knew what I was doing, Callie Mae."

"Did you know the pinto was going to circle around to fight you, too?" she demanded. "To make sure you'd stay away from his mares?"

TJ hesitated. *That* he hadn't expected. The stallion had come from nowhere and was unrelenting in his attack. Blue had defended them both as best he could, but TJ had heard the terror in the thoroughbred's screams.

"I should have," he admitted.

His glance lifted to the sight of his precious horse, tied to brush beside his buckskin and Callie Mae's roan. Safe. Calmed. In the quiet of the canyon, the manada long gone, relief poured through TJ.

He'd had his hands full keeping his seat on Blue while the two stallions tangled. After TJ had been thrown and knocked cold, Blue could have bolted, and TJ wouldn't have known until it was too late…

But Callie Mae had been there. She'd kept Blue from running again.

He returned his gaze to her, her face only inches away from his. A fine layer of dust coated her skin, clung to the tips of her lashes. Eyes the color of a summer sky peered up at him with somber intensity.

"He's yours again, TJ," she said.

"Yes."

He heard no animosity in the hushed tone of her voice. Only understanding, as if she'd come to accept why the horse meant so much to him, despite their differences of opinion on it.

"Guess I've got you to thank for that," he added in a low murmur.

Wind-strewn wisps lay across her forehead and brow. It wasn't often anyone saw Callie Mae Lockett like he saw her now, with her high-society airs forgotten, her defenses down. When every hair on her head wasn't swept upward and topped with fancy millinery that cost more than any woman should dare to pay.

This was the side of her she was born to be. The Lockett side. A woman whose legacy would forever bind her to the land and its essence. One who needed the wind to color her cheeks and brighten her eyes and veil her skin with the clean scent of air and sun.

A woman who, like himself, craved the land, needed to be close to it to survive.

TJ savored the sight of her laying in the dirt and rough range grass, in her borrowed shirt and denims, cinnamon curls tangled and errant.

His fingers smoothed them away from her face. That he had the privilege—and she hadn't protested—filled him with a slow yearning he didn't bother to bank.

A yearning for more.

Her breasts snuggled against his chest; he pressed closer, to feel them more fully. He detected the faintest hitch in her breathing, her acknowledgement of what he'd done. And why. Her sky-blue orbs turned dark, sultry. A kinship of their thoughts.

His gaze drifted along the proud line of her nose and settled over her mouth. A glorious mouth, dusky, perfectly shaped.

Meant to be enjoyed by a man.

"Kiss me, TJ," she whispered, watching him. "Being's that's what we're both thinking about right now."

The fire in his loins leapt through his blood. No shy female, this one. She knew what she wanted and went after it. At some point, growing up, she'd learned how it was between a man and a woman. The pleasures to be found.

Had Kullen taught her?

The thought haunted TJ. Yet he gave no consideration to wanting what belonged to another, not when he'd wanted Callie Mae himself for so long.

And she was here, now. Beneath him and in his arms. His head lowered, and he touched his mouth to hers, the fear in him real that he was only imagining this moment. Dreamed it as he had so many times before.

The softness of her lips, their warmth and sweetness, assured him this was no trick of his mind.

His head lifted. Growing lust swirled through him, a need to make the moment last, to take from Callie Mae what he craved and she seemed willing to give.

Sheer control kept him from it.

He wanted too much.

She couldn't know how much.

Her lashes lifted. She gazed up at him, her scrutiny searching, as if she questioned his restraint.

Then, clearly dismissing it, her arms slid up his shoulders, hooked around his neck. And tugged.

"Another," she commanded softly.

His control broke. He growled her name and took her mouth with a savagery of unleashed desire, too long held in check while he lived his life in the shadows of her legacy. In her being a Lockett.

It didn't matter that he was only a cowboy on the sprawling C Bar C, that he'd watched her grow up with scores of others on the ranch, all of them, from the outside looking in. And it didn't matter how much she'd hated him for what she believed he'd done, that he'd given too many months of his life behind bars.

It didn't matter. Not anymore.

He was man; she was woman. And they both had this fiery *need.*

TJ shifted his body, angled his head, fisted his hand in her hair. He deepened the kiss, prolonged it, feeding the need which demanded to be quenched. Her mouth opened, eager and hungry, and their tongues met. Mated, hot and frenzied. Their breaths turned rough, aching—

TJ had always known Callie Mae would be a vibrant, sensual woman, but this, *this* shattered any control, any shred of restraint he was honor bound to maintain. He hungered for more, to discover every sweet inch of this woman who'd inspired his longings and invaded his every thought for more years than he cared to count. His hand slid over her ribs to take the delectable weight of her breast into his palm.

A purring moan slipped from her throat, and she pressed her hips into his, discovering the thickening evidence of his lust, demanding to be sated.

TJ trailed rasping kisses down her cheek, over her jaw, onto the warm curve of her neck. His fingers parted the buttons of her shirt, spread the fabric wide and bared the rounded globe of flesh that set his blood on fire all over again.

Craving this new taste of her, he closed his lips over one erect nipple and traced its shape with his tongue. He suckled and savored. Her back arched, her fingers spread into his hair, holding him to her—

Suddenly, she stilled.

Then, before he could even *think* it, her legs flailed and she cried out in dismay.

"No, no. Get off me!" she gasped and pushed at his shoulders. "Stop kissing me like that. Oh, stop!"

"Callie Mae." He blinked down at her. His lust-drugged mind scrambled to comprehend her sudden change in thinking. "Darlin'."

"Don't 'darlin'' me, TJ Grier. Get off!"

With more agility than he could've thought possible,

she darted out from beneath him and scurried to her feet, holding the edges of her shirt tightly closed. Sucking in an anguished breath, she whirled away, and in the time it took for him to sit up and rake a frustrated hand through his hair, she turned back, her shirt fastened in an untidy match of buttons to their holes.

She squared her shoulders, lifted her chin. And swallowed.

"Forgive me," she said, her voice unsteady. "I should never have allowed—such a thing to happen."

Acutely aware the swelling in his groin remained an ache that needed assuaging, he stood, too. "Don't make it sound as if we were doing something dirty."

"It was wrong, TJ." Pride kept her gaze from wavering. "I'm engaged to be married to Kullen. I shouldn't have been k-kissing you like I was."

"You think you betrayed him?"

"I know I did."

TJ took a step toward her, the need to take her into his arms, make her forget again, consuming.

"And yet what you were feeling, Callie Mae, was passion—for me," he said softly.

"No." She took a step back and shook her head. Emphatically. "No, it wasn't."

"Don't deny it."

His taunt jerked her chin a notch higher. "I'll not deny I got swept away by the moment. In all the excitement of chasing after Blue and then thinking you were hurt, well, my emotions got—" she hesitated "—mixed up."

"Mixed up."

"But I'm thinking more clearly now."

"Are you?" He dared another step.

She held up a hand to stop him. "You have your horse, TJ. There's no reason for me to stay with you. I'm going back to Amarillo. This time, you can't stop me."

Pivoting, she rushed toward the tethered mounts, and he hurried after her.

"What about Danny, Callie Mae?" he demanded. "Isn't finding the truth about his death important anymore?"

"I have every intention of discussing it with Kullen."

He snorted in derision. "You really think he'll talk?"

She swung toward him in exasperation. "I have to start somewhere, TJ!"

They halted near the horses, and he set his hands on his hips. Given her devotion to the man, TJ understood her determination to see him. How could TJ keep her from leaving? How could he convince her that she needed the truth as much as he did, and that they needed each other to find it?

"I'm going with you," he said firmly.

"To see Kullen?"

"Yes, to see Kullen," he snapped. "So I can choke the information out of him if I have to."

He stepped toward Blue to take hold of his rope, and if Callie Mae protested his intentions, sheer horror kept him from hearing the words.

Blood seeped from an ugly slash across Blue's belly, and TJ realized he wasn't going anywhere soon.

* * *

Emmett Ralston stared hard at the coffeepot.

Strange how it lay there, knocked over like it was. As if someone had thrown it—or kicked it—even though it looked plain as day that they intended to make some brew. An open tin of Arbuckles lay right there by the fire, which had long since died out.

His gaze shifted to the pair of bedrolls, laying side by side, all rumpled. The two Stetsons, one smaller than the other, lying near saddlebags.

No one would leave their hats behind, unless they left in one hell of a hurry.

He dismounted, squatted next to the saddlebags and dumped out their contents. Among them, a small purse, brown velvet with a gold chain. On the outside, monogrammed in gold thread, was a likeness of the C Bar C brand.

He grunted at the discovery, opened the purse and found a small roll of bills. Quickly, he stuffed the wad into his shirt pocket and tossed the velvet bag aside. The rest of the supplies held no interest.

Rising again, he swept a glance around him. Far as he could tell, there was no sign of an ambush, but it was clear he'd found Grier's camp and that the Lockett woman had been with him.

Maybe their leaving had something to do with Blue Whistler. Then again, maybe not. Either way, by the looks of that cold fire, they'd been gone a while.

Emmett squinted an eye toward the sky. A few more hours and it'd be dark. He could either keep searching for them or he could stay and wait for them to return.

Gut instinct told him they'd be back. Only fools would roam the range without supplies to sustain them.

And TJ Grier was no fool.

He knew something about the night Danny died. Emmett didn't know what, or how much, but TJ had hired a big-city agent to investigate the boy's death and help Grier clear his name. Emmett knew it for sure; he'd overheard Boomer and Grier talking back at the Preston stables when they didn't know he was around.

Which was why Kullen needed Grier dead in a hurry.

They both did.

To stop him—and the Lockett woman—from learning the truth.

Kullen had been as mad as a cut cat when he found out Callie Mae's brother was killed. It hadn't been part of their plan for him to die. Emmett's job had been to kidnap him, that's all. Use him for a healthy ransom as part of their plan for revenge against Penn McClure.

Emmett had to talk fast to convince Kullen it wasn't his fault the kid died. That that crazy drunk was responsible, but when he up and disappeared, and Grier claimed to kill the boy by accident, well, things got easier and Kullen felt a whole lot better.

Happy, as a matter of fact.

Kullen Brockway—Brosius, Emmett corrected himself—was as fine a lawyer as could be found. Shrewd and calculated, just like one should be. If anyone could get back at Penn McClure for what he'd done, killing Kullen's old man, Kullen could.

He deserved as much C Bar C money as he could get for all he'd lost, and marrying Callie Mae Lockett would get him plenty. Once them two got married, Emmett would be set for life. Kullen had promised, and Emmett could hardly wait to head south across the border and find himself a little Mexican beauty…

Except Kullen being crippled changed things, and now it was up to Emmett to see their plan through. Kill TJ Grier and bring Callie Mae back to Kullen where she belonged.

Emmett mounted up and headed toward a stand of junipers where he could keep an eye on the camp without Grier knowing it.

Then, when the time was right, he'd make his move.

Chapter Eleven

Every bone, every muscle in Callie Mae's body ached.

After leaving the box canyon, they'd ridden slowly back to the stream where the herd had earlier stopped to water. TJ had submerged the stallion in the stream's cold depths to stop the belly wound's bleeding. With nothing to suture the gash, they'd been forced to return to camp at a careful walk.

Made a long day even longer, for sure. Worse, she had too much time to think.

About TJ.

About the kisses they'd shared.

About the words pounding over and over in her head: *what you were feeling, Callie Mae, was passion—for me.*

TJ had been wrong, of course. She was young, healthy, female. What he'd made her feel was merely lust at its most basic level.

Nothing personal involved.

She blamed it on the thrill of infiltrating the wild horses with him. When before had she had such an opportunity? TJ's mastery over the herd had seemed effortless; and the way he flaunted the danger, well, the experience was as far-flung from the sedate life she normally led as could be, that's all. When TJ had fallen and scared her, then held her in his arms...

His kisses had proved his expertise in seducing a woman, and like a fool, she'd fallen beneath his spell. How could she have allowed herself? How could she have completely forgotten she belonged to another man?

Her behavior had been inexcusable.

Well, it wouldn't happen again. Ever.

But she could feel TJ's gaze on her often during the day's ride, and it was all she could do to keep from meeting those dark eyes. His silence, her own troubled thoughts, made the hours interminable.

Why she didn't just up and leave him, follow through on her threat to return to Amarillo, she couldn't fathom. Something held her back. Something that had to do with him fending for himself with an injured horse in tow...and his desperate need to find the truth in Danny's death.

A need that equaled hers.

I'm going with you.

I'll choke the information out of him if I have to.

TJ's continual insistence that the man she planned to marry was involved sent confusion throbbing inside Callie Mae's head.

She swallowed a miserable groan. Handsome, intelligent Kullen. It didn't seem possible he could be capable of a crime as terrible as scheming to hurt a child, and yet...yet his startling behavior at Preston Farm had been most vindictive.

Was TJ correct in his suspicions?

She had no choice but to concede TJ accompanying her to see Kullen was the smart thing to do. If TJ managed to wreak any kind of admission out of Kullen, Callie Mae had to be there to hear it—for Danny's sake.

Mother would expect it of her, besides.

And *that* thought had her thinking of her meeting with the entrepreneurs and how everything took a tailspin turn for the worse as soon as she left the Amarillo Hotel. How was she going to prove herself to her parents, if she was out here on the Texas range chasing mustangs and rescuing an injured racehorse, with TJ Grier, of all people?

"Hell of a frown you're wearing, Callie Mae," he said.

Her ruminating ended with a start, and she realized they'd reached their camp. She pulled up, refusing to look at him.

"Yes, well, I have a lot on my mind."

"We both do." He dismounted. "Want to talk about it?"

"Not particularly." She looped the reins around the saddle horn and swung off her mount, taking a moment to allow her stiff muscles to loosen. By the time they did, TJ had moved to her side, crowding her between the span of their horses.

"Listen, Callie Mae," he said in a low voice. "What happened back there between us—"

"Should never have happened," she snapped and angled her body to escape him.

But his hand clasped her elbow, stopping her, making her aware of the warm strength in his grip.

"Well, it did, and now it's scaring you," he said. "Because I made you feel something you're not used to feeling. Isn't that right?"

"Yes!" She steeled herself against how ruthless he looked with his cheeks roughened by the day's stubble, his expression dark and fierce. "You made me feel guilt, TJ, for allowing you privileges that no—that I've never given—"

His brow shot up. "No one?"

Her breasts tingled at the memory of his kisses; their dusky tips relived the feel of his hot, wet tongue over them, and God, she hated to admit he'd been the first to kiss her like that. Gritting her teeth, she angled her face away.

"No," she said.

A moment passed. Then, lean fingers cupped her chin and turned her back to face him.

"How could he keep his hands off you, Callie Mae?" he demanded, his tone husky. "He must have ice in his veins."

Kullen's reserved manner had troubled her at times, but she'd always found an excuse for it, telling herself some men were more adept at showing their affections than others. Once they were married, he'd change. She'd show him how desirable she could be in their marital bed, and he'd be happy to have her as his wife.

"Kullen is a gentleman," she grated. "He's never stepped across the bounds of propriety. He loves and respects me too much."

TJ snorted in derision. "I told you, he loves and respects your money more."

She stiffened against the slur and the unexpected sting of tears which followed. TJ's contempt had turned wearing; if she wasn't careful, she might find herself *believing* all the hateful things he said about Kullen.

"I'm going to make some coffee. Excuse me," she said, pushing past him.

He let her go, and grateful, she busied herself building a fire. She took comfort from the task and tried hard to keep from giving TJ's comments further thought. Even though she made a steadfast attempt to ignore him, her ear kept tuned to his movements behind her and the low croon of his voice as he unsaddled the horses and hobbled them.

With the flames blazing, she rose to retrieve the coffeepot and fill it with water. Only then, did she notice the items scattered over the ground, dumped out of the saddlebags.

Her attention snagged on her brown velvet purse with its gold chain. Callie Mae hadn't touched the little bag since leaving Stinky Dale's last night. A quick check revealed the money inside gone, and the hairs on the back of her neck prickled.

"Someone's been here, TJ," she said, turning to him.

"What?" He straightened from examining Blue's injury and cast her a distracted glance.

"While we were gone, someone rode into our camp and rummaged through our things." She held up the purse. "He stole my money."

TJ scowled, and he joined her. "Anything else missing?"

She ran a mental check over the supplies Stinky Dale had given them. Tins of beans, sardines, hardtack. The tin of Arbuckles hadn't been touched. Neither had their bedrolls or even their Stetsons.

"I don't think so," she said, annoyance building that the stranger had left her penniless. Now she'd have to make time for a trip to the bank in Amarillo to replenish the funds. "Who do you suppose it was?"

"No way to know for sure." TJ squatted and dipped his fingers into markings in the dirt. "The tracks aren't very old. One horse, one rider, though." Rising, he examined the ground around them.

"A drifter, maybe?"

"I doubt it. He would've helped himself to our food and whatever else he could find, besides your money." He met her gaze. "Whoever he was, he took the time to cover his tracks out of here. So we couldn't follow him."

The troubled light in his leather-brown eyes worried her.

"What are you thinking?" she asked, fighting alarm.

"I'm thinking that little frippery you got there told the rider what he wanted to know."

Her glance dropped to her purse, then lifted again. Understanding dawned, but she hoped she was wrong. "Meaning?"

"Meaning your brand sewn real pretty on that velvet made it clear who owned it."

By now, gossip would be rampant in Amarillo—and beyond—about what happened at Preston Farm. Folks would know TJ had put a gun to her head and forced her to run with him to chase down Blue. They might even have sympathy for Kullen and the way he acted, thinking he tried to defend her.

More troubling, once word reached the C Bar C, given TJ's tarnished reputation among the outfit, they were sure to be alarmed.

"Maybe someone from the ranch is looking for me," she said, regretting their worry if it were true. She had, after all, come to no harm with TJ.

His glance turned skeptical. "And steal your money when they found you?"

"No." Immediately, she discarded the idea. "You're right. Of course not."

Every man in her outfit, loyal to a fault, could be trusted. None of them would dream of taking anything from her without her permission.

Would they?

"Whoever it was, it's strange they didn't stay here and wait for me to come back," she said instead.

TJ's mouth quirked. "Exactly."

She resisted what he implied, that something illicit could be happening. "Maybe you're wrong. Maybe it was just someone down on their luck and looking for money. When they found mine, they simply took it."

His dark eyes didn't waver from hers. "Guess we could 'maybe' all night long, couldn't we, Callie Mae?"

Her apprehension grew. "You're thinking Kullen has something to do with this, aren't you?"

A muscle in his jaw leapt, as if he could hardly hold in his contempt for the man.

"All I'm saying is your whereabouts is information that could be important to someone, and we both know Kullen would be at the top of the list," he said. "Until I know who tracked you here, *if* someone tracked you here, I don't want you out of my sight."

She crossed her arms and shivered. "You're scaring me, TJ."

"I don't mean to." He chucked her under the chin. "Just don't wander off."

He pivoted toward the horses, but at the sound of approaching hoofbeats, he turned back. Sure the intruder had returned, Callie Mae sucked in a quick breath and took an instinctive step closer to TJ.

He circled his arm around her shoulders and pulled her against him in a reassuring movement so casual, so automatic, he didn't seem to realize what he'd done.

"Well, I'll be damned," he breathed. "It's Boomer and Maggie."

"Yes," she murmured, her surprise great but not enough to mask her awareness of TJ's body next to hers. "Looks like Stinky Dale is with them."

"That's him, all right."

Boomer leading, the trio rode closer.

"We were hopin' that campfire was yours," the

horseman said. "You're a sight for sore eyes, TJ, let me tell you."

TJ grinned. "Could say the same about you." They drew up and TJ indicated the white cotton sling which protected the man's arm, a grim reminder of how Kullen had shot him only yesterday. "How're you doing?"

"Well enough, I reckon." He shrugged one shoulder. "Bullet took out a piece of my hide. Hurts like the dickens, but I'll live."

"He refused to stay at the farm." Maggie spoke up in her quiet voice. "You all right, son?"

Their looks connected. "Better than when I saw you last."

Her gaze dragged to Callie Mae and touched on TJ's arm, still draped around her shoulders. Seeing it, too, Boomer frowned beneath his white moustache. Maggie bit her lip and quickly averted her eyes. Even Stinky Dale's brows furrowed beneath the brim of his Stetson.

Tension built in the air, thick enough to cut. Callie Mae took a smooth step away from TJ, and his arm dropped back to his side.

Little wonder his mother appeared upset, she supposed. Maggie wouldn't approve of TJ having much of anything to do with Callie Mae, and after what happened at Boomer's, Callie Mae couldn't much blame her. The woman was just too timid to say or do anything about it.

Regret twirled through Callie Mae. She'd known Maggie Grier for years. Poor thing had had her share of personal troubles, but she was a hard worker, and her employment on the C Bar C as bunkhouse cook had been an honest one.

Except for yesterday, Callie Mae hadn't seen her since Danny died; she'd been strangely absent during TJ's trial and afterward.

But Callie Mae reminded herself that her grudge against TJ had nothing to do with his mother. Or Boomer, either, for that matter, whose loyalty to both of them was obvious.

Suddenly, it became important to set them at ease and assure them she wasn't the vindictive shrew they thought she was.

Callie Mae managed a smile. "I was just going to make coffee. I'm sure you could all use some. It won't take me long."

Acutely aware of their eyes upon her, especially TJ's, she stepped away to attend to the task.

TJ turned his attention to Stinky Dale. "How'd you manage to hook up with Boomer and Maggie?"

"After you and Miss Lockett left our place last night, I couldn't stop thinking about you two out on the range, looking for a horse you had no guarantee of finding. Figured you could use some help. I decided then and there to ride over to Boomer's and see if he'd like to come along."

TJ nodded. "Glad you did."

"Makes two of us." Then, Boomer exclaimed. "I'll be damned, TJ. Is that Blue I'm lookin' at?"

"It is."

Heads turned toward the three tethered horses, tails

flicking, their long noses bent to the grass. The thoroughbred's midnight black hide, his elegance and power, set him apart from the other two.

"Woo-wee!" Boomer grinned. "Reckon we're too late."

Stinky Dale slid a low whistle between his teeth. "Isn't he something!"

"A little worse for wear, I'm afraid," TJ said with a sigh. "He tangled with the lead stallion in that herd of mustangs you told me about."

"You found him with 'em, then?" The cowboy swung out of the saddle to join Boomer, already down.

"I'd still be looking if you hadn't mentioned them." Appreciation threaded TJ's voice.

"He got roughed up some, did he?" One-handed, Boomer flipped open a saddlebag. "I was afraid something like that might happen, the way he got his freedom handed to him so fast. I brought my vet kit, just in case."

"He got cut on the belly," TJ said, his voice filled with relief. "I didn't have anything to sew him up with."

"Let's take a look at him."

Boomer hustled off, Stinky Dale on his heels. TJ moved toward Maggie, but she'd already dismounted by the time he got there to help.

"Have you had your supper yet?" she asked.

"We just got back with Blue." He patted his lean stomach. "But we're starved. Neither of us had anything to eat today."

"Nothing?" She darted a hesitant glance at Callie

Mae. "Go on and tend to your horse, then, and I'll stir something up. We'll talk later."

He regarded her. "I'm glad you're here, but it wasn't necessary, Maggie."

"I couldn't stay away."

"I know." He bent and pressed a kiss to her cheek. "Make plenty of grub for us, then, all right?"

Suddenly, she enveloped him in a quick hug. "I was worried about you with her, TJ."

Though Maggie kept her voice low, Callie Mae's listening picked up the words, and she stiffened. She couldn't hear TJ's response, and she told herself she didn't want to.

It was silly to feel hurt, but she did. Callie Mae kept herself busy adding coffee to the pot she'd filled with water; she studiously set it over the fire to boil.

By the time she straightened, TJ had joined Boomer and Stinky Dale, and Maggie stood in front of her, clutching a wicker hamper to her chest, as if she needed to hold on to the thing for courage.

Several inches shorter, she had to tilt her head back to meet Callie Mae's gaze beneath her hat brim; though her skin showed signs of her age, her chestnut-colored eyes were clear.

The sight struck Callie Mae.

The whiskey which used to cloud those eyes was gone.

"Hello, Maggie," she said quietly.

"Miss Lockett." Her throat moved. "Miss Lockett, there's something I have to say."

"I'm happy to listen." Callie Mae sought to put the woman at ease and gave her a small smile.

"My son—TJ—" She drew in a quavery breath; moisture formed beneath her lashes. "He's been hurt real bad with everything's that happened, and he deserved none of it, so I'm just askin' that you leave him alone. You and Mr. Brosius. Please."

Callie Mae didn't move. "I do believe TJ's troubles were of his own doing."

With the exception of Blue Whistler's spooking back at Preston Farm, of course. And *that* had been Emmett Ralston's doing, with Kullen a puzzling part of it, but the root of the matter trailed back to Danny's dying, which TJ had admitted responsibility—

"You don't know that. You don't," Maggie insisted.

"Oh?" Callie Mae's brow arched. "Would you care to enlighten me on what I'm ignorant of?"

Maggie's gaze dropped. Her lips pressed together. Her expression turned pale and anguished, and like a thunderbolt, realization flashed through Callie Mae.

Maggie Grier knew something that was tearing her apart.

"Maggie?" Callie Mae fisted her hand to keep from touching her. As much as the woman despised her, she wouldn't appreciate the gesture. "What is it?"

Maggie's head came up. "Just leave my son alone, will you? Go back to your fancy ranch and never come back!"

Chin quivering, she set the wicker hamper down with a heavy thud and flew like a frightened bird to join the men by the horses.

Callie Mae stared after her. What had she kept herself from saying? Something so terrible she couldn't speak the words?

Instinct told Callie Mae they were words she needed to hear, and somehow, she had to find a way to unlock the secret Maggie kept hidden inside her.

Chapter Twelve

"You're going to have to pull him out of the Fort Worth race," Boomer said, the timbre of his voice unusually somber. "You know that, don't you?"

TJ dragged in deep on his cigarette and held the smoke in his lungs. Bitter disappointment rolled through him. He exhaled slowly and nodded. "Yeah."

"Damned shame." Stinky Dale shook his head and cupped his hand around the match flame.

TJ squinted through the smoke of their collective cigarettes and fastened his gaze on the stream meandering along the edge of their camp. Moonlight glistened on the tranquil water, a sight that would've been soothing if his gut hadn't been so tied up in knots.

Supper had come and gone. Maggie had filled their bellies with her rib-sticking chili and corn muffins left over from yesterday's baking. Now, they'd let their meals settle while she and Callie Mae cleaned up.

"Could've been worse, I suppose," he muttered, but took little comfort from his own logic.

Stinky Dale nodded. "He could've gone lame or something."

TJ shot him a scowl. "Don't even think that, Stinky. Let alone say it."

The cowboy shrugged. "It's true."

TJ knew it was. He just wasn't of a mind to admit it.

"He'll heal well enough," Boomer added. "Just going to take some time, that's all."

Time TJ didn't have. He'd already spent his winnings—in his mind at least. He'd been that sure Blue would triumph in the race down south. The days and weeks he and Boomer, Maggie and Lodi spent training, planning, hoping—hell, all of them were sure.

Now, he'd go a little deeper into debt, a little more beholden to Boomer. A lot more impatient to get himself on track to respectability again.

Would he ever get there? Would his life never get better? Easier? Successful?

Most frustrating of all, though, TJ was nowhere closer to finding the truth in Danny's death. How could he convince Callie Mae to stay with him for as long as it took, so he could?

Now that he'd found Blue, she was even more determined to return to Kullen. Hell, she'd probably be itching to go back to the C Bar C, too. Take a hot bath, change clothes. Her life there waited for her. Comfort and responsibilities. The outfit, maybe even her parents, would be concerned by her absence.

The list went on and on.

Time. He was just about out of it.

Worse, someone was looking for her. Or him. Probably both of them. Didn't take a genius to figure the person was most likely Emmett Ralston, working for Kullen while the bastard was laid up.

Tendrils of panic curled through TJ. Once Callie Mae left him, he wouldn't be able to stop her from getting married. He wouldn't be able to watch out for her. He wouldn't know if something happened, if she got hurt or scared—

Until it was too late.

And something *would* happen. He could feel it. His gaze shifted to the darkness beyond the camp, their fire a beacon to anyone in the shadows.

TJ had informed Maggie, Boomer and Stinky Dale about the intruder, that whoever it was had found Callie Mae's brown velvet purse, emblazoned with her brand. Their thinking concurred with his. They had to act on the assumption the thief, by his absence, was up to no good.

"He's watching us," TJ said, his voice subdued to keep from reaching his mother and Callie Mae.

Boomer pulled his gaze off Blue. His lips tightened. "Reckon so."

"We're like sitting ducks out here."

"Maybe we should saddle up, take a look around," Stinky said.

"He'd see us." TJ discarded the idea; he'd already been tempted to do just that, but with no tracks to follow, and the night black as pitch, they'd be wasting their efforts. "He's got the advantage, hiding in the dark."

Stinky studied the burning end of his cigarette. "*If* he is."

"We have to presume it."

Boomer sighed. "Could be a long night."

TJ studied his friend. In the shadows cast by the firelight, the older man's skin shone pale, his expression fatigued. The wounding he'd suffered yesterday clearly taking its toll.

"Best if we take turns as guard," Stinky Dale said.

"Good idea." Boomer nodded.

"I have a better one," TJ said and ground out his cigarette in the dirt.

"Yeah?" the other two said in unison.

"Get Blue out of here. Take him home under cover of darkness. I can't risk someone trying to hurt him or steal him."

"Tonight?" Stinky Dale asked, surprised.

"That's right."

Oblivious to their discussion, Maggie headed past them on the way to the stream, carrying the chili kettle for washing. Once she was out of earshot, TJ continued.

"I want my mother out of here, too. She scares easy. It'd be hard on her if anything happens."

Boomer finished his smoking. "That it would."

Thinking of the day's ride his friend had already ridden, and another one just like it ahead of him, TJ endured a new worry. "You up to it, Boomer?"

He scowled. "Don't make me sound as if I've got one foot in the grave."

TJ took no offense at his gruffness. "You've had a rough time of it."

"Not so rough that I can't do what you're askin'."

"If you're sure."

"I am."

"What would you like me to do?" Stinky Dale asked.

TJ swiveled his glance toward the cowboy. "Go with Maggie and Boomer. Help them with Blue."

Keep them safe.

"You can count on it," he said.

His loyalty meant the world to TJ. Stinky Dale had proven to be one of the few good things he'd taken away from his years at the C Bar C.

Right along with a foolish love for Callie Mae.

TJ found her across the campfire, packing clean silverware into Maggie's wicker hamper. Her braid was a charming mess, and she had to pause to tuck loose strands behind one ear before resuming her work. She'd rolled up her cuffs to wash the dishes, revealing slender, feminine arms—

He knew the feel of those arms around him, how they'd held her body pressed to his. The memory rushed back, ignited a slow fire inside him, one that never seemed to go away. Made him forget where he was—

The crunch of footsteps reminded him in a hurry. Maggie, coming back from the stream, the clean kettle dripping at her side.

She passed the three of them without seeming to

notice they were there. Her troubled expression told TJ her mind was at it again. Plaguing her with worries and fears and the haunting grief which never left her.

"I'd like to marry her, TJ, when this is all over," Boomer said quietly.

Pleasure distracted his concerns, and TJ gave him a lopsided grin. "You asking my permission, old man?"

"Just wanted you to know."

TJ's grin faded. He studied Maggie again. "She'll think she's not good enough for you."

"I know." Boomer's glance lingered over her, too, for a long moment. "And she won't say yes until she's got you taken care of."

TJ grunted, knowing it.

"You're all she's got," the horseman said. "She figures she owes you. Considering everything that's happened."

"This thing is my problem." And had been since the night Danny died. "I don't need her help to fix it."

Suddenly impatient, he rose. The other two stood with him.

"Let's get going," he said and approached the campfire.

Callie Mae latched the hamper and glanced up at him. In the flames' light, her eyes appeared black, heavily lashed. Curious.

"I'm sending Boomer home with Blue," he said.

"Now?" she asked, taken aback.

"Yes. He can tend to Blue better at the farm. They both need to rest, besides."

She stood, faced him. "But it's late, TJ."

"Stinky Dale is going with them," he said, not budging.

Her glance slid to the cowboy, then back to TJ.

"All right," she said slowly.

"You'll come with us, won't you, TJ?" Maggie asked.

"No." At her instant alarm, he softened. "But soon," he added.

"This has to do with the rider who broke into our camp, doesn't it?" Callie Mae asked.

"I don't want to take any chances on him stealing Blue."

"Do you know something you're not telling me?"

He stilled at her query.

For one wild moment, he thought she spoke of what he'd done. His part in Danny's death.

But in the next, he realized she didn't mean that at all.

Relief swept through him. He chose his words carefully. "I haven't seen anything, Callie Mae. If I did, I'd tell you."

Even after he'd said the words, he wondered if they were true. Would he only want to protect her? Figure what she didn't know wouldn't hurt her?

"Let's load up, Maggie," Boomer said. "The night's not getting any younger."

"I'll give you a hand with that hamper," Stinky Dale said, right behind him.

"You agreed to leaving like this, Boomer?" Maggie demanded, not moving. "Now?"

"I did. We got to take care of Blue."

"We need to take care of TJ *more*," she insisted.

It wasn't often she resisted a decision TJ and Boomer made together. That she did so now showed a glimmer of the spirit she hadn't shown in much too long.

But TJ had no intention of letting her stay.

"I'll feel better when you're all safe at home, Maggie," he said.

"What about *your* safety? Or hers?" She gestured stiffly toward Callie Mae.

"I'll take care of us," he said simply.

"C'mon, Maggie." Boomer's gentle-but-firm tug pulled her away from the hamper, so he and Stinky Dale could carry it toward the horses.

Except Callie Mae moved in front of it.

So they couldn't.

Feet spread, chin high, jaw set, she looked just like her mother standing there. Proud and defiant. In control. Capable of carrying on her legacy and defending it.

The sight of her stirred TJ's admiration.

And his unease.

"No one is going anywhere," she said coolly. "Until I find out exactly what happened the night Danny died."

No one spoke.

Callie Mae kept her expression blank, but her heart pounded in her ears.

What if she was wrong? What if her instincts had overreacted to Maggie's mental sensitivities?

Time pounded away, right along with her heart. After Maggie rode off with Boomer into the night, the opportunity would be lost for Callie Mae to demand the answers she needed from the woman. Who knew when Callie Mae would get another chance?

Again and again, TJ insisted there was more to learn, more than she knew. That his trial, the evidence, had failed to reveal the truth.

She had to risk looking stupid and being wrong. Maybe she'd misjudged Maggie's furtive looks all through supper. Her nervousness. But there had to be a reason for the way she acted and, for tonight at least, no one could blame it on whiskey.

"I told you, Callie Mae." TJ slid her a smooth smile. "We'll get to that when we talk to Kullen."

"His side of it, yes. If he talks." Her own mouth crooked. "And we both know that'll be a big *if,* don't we?"

The admission startled her, as if her subconscious had pushed the thought out of her mind and onto her tongue. Kullen's actions at Preston Farm had revealed his malice toward TJ, the depth of which he'd clearly gone to great lengths to conceal from Callie Mae.

"Oh, he'll talk, all right," TJ said softly. With some malice of his own.

Unfortunately, Callie Mae wasn't so sure Kullen would. Not anymore. Her glance swung to Maggie. The woman quickly averted her eyes and her throat moved, as if she'd swallowed down a response.

"Maggie?" Callie Mae said quietly. "Is there something you'd like to say?"

"Reckon talking can come later, Miss Lockett,"

Boomer said, his voice loud in the woman's silence. "She's had a long day. We all have. C'mon, Maggie. We've got to get going." He stepped forward and took her elbow with his good hand.

"Let her speak for herself, Boomer," Callie Mae ordered.

TJ grasped Maggie's other elbow. "Boomer's right, Callie Mae. It's getting late, and they've got a long ride ahead of them. Grab that hamper, will you, Stinky Dale?"

Not waiting to see if he did, TJ and Boomer turned, taking Maggie, keeping her sandwiched between them. Their haste couldn't have been more obvious than if they'd thrown her over their shoulders and *ran* toward the horses.

Instant suspicion curled through Callie Mae, but before she could demand they stop, Maggie suddenly yanked free of their grips.

"No!" she cried out. She pressed her fingertips to her temples and squeezed her eyes closed. Her thin body trembled.

The poor woman seemed on the brink. Of something. Callie Mae held her breath.

Choking back a sob, Maggie opened her eyes and appealed to TJ with a tormented expression.

"I can't keep on like this," she said hoarsely.

"Like what?" Callie Mae asked, taking a step toward her. "What has made you so unhappy?"

"Don't say anything, Maggie." TJ reached for her. She evaded him. "I have to tell her."

"You're tired, honey." Boomer reached for her, too, with the same result. "You're—"

"Don't make excuses for me, Boomer." She drew in a quavery breath. "It doesn't help. It never helps."

"I'm speakin' the truth this time, so—"

Callie Mae held up a hand. "Enough, Boomer. Let her talk."

The horseman exchanged a troubled glance with TJ, who tightened his lips and clenched his fists and stood very, very still.

"Maggie." TJ cleared his throat. "Maggie, don't do it."

"I have to." She straightened her back, pivoted on her boot heel and faced Callie Mae square. "I've got something to say to you, Miss Lockett. And when I do, I want you to know it's the truth. Leastways, I'll go to my grave believin' it is."

"Certainly, Maggie." Callie Mae marveled at how calm she sounded when her heart started pounding all over again. "I'm listening."

"It's about your brother. Little Danny. He—I—" Her slim throat worked, and a shimmer of tears shone in her dark eyes, saddle-leather brown and so much like her son's. "I killed him, Miss Lockett. It was me. Not TJ."

Callie Mae's world tilted. Her fingers flew to her lips, stifling her shocked gasp. Whatever she might have thought Maggie would say, it hadn't been this.

Never this.

"What?" she choked.

TJ breathed a vehement curse and raked his hand

through his hair. Stinky Dale studied the toes of his boots. And Boomer just looked miserable.

"I was there that night, in the new horse barn, when Danny came looking for TJ," she said.

"You were?" Callie Mae rasped. "Why?"

It would've been late, she recalled. The night of her welcome-home party. Danny had been at the house, among the guests, until nearly midnight. Callie Mae had seen him herself and talked to him, as had so many others.

But then he'd disappeared.

And no one had noticed.

Until it was too late.

"I needed whiskey." Maggie whispered the words, but she seemed to gain strength from them. "I had more," she added, her voice stronger. "Another bottle in TJ's office."

Callie Mae nodded slowly. "Go on."

"Danny walked in, looking for TJ, calling for him. Then *he* came. Out of the dark. He said he'd take Danny to see TJ."

"Who, Maggie?" Callie Mae demanded. "*Who* was waiting in the dark?"

For the barest of moments, the other woman's chin quivered. "I don't know. I never saw him before. He wore his hat over his eyes, real low, but his voice, the way he acted—I didn't recognize him."

"Were you drunk?" Callie Mae couldn't help the accusation threading through her voice. "Maybe you knew him but don't remember it. Maybe he was C Bar C. Someone in the outfit. Or maybe this was all a figment of your imagination because the whiskey was messing with your mind."

"I'd been drinking, yes. But I could smell trouble when it was happening."

Callie Mae tried not to feel skeptical. Maggie's reputation for imbibing spirits had been well-known through the years. "What happened next?"

"He tried to steal Danny."

"Steal him? You mean, kidnap him?"

"Yes."

"Oh, my God."

"But Danny, he acted fast and threw the lantern at him, then I hit the stranger on the head with my whiskey bottle and told Danny to run. He did, and by then the fire started. The stranger threw me off and went chasing after him. I ran for TJ's shotgun and when I found them, the stranger almost had Danny, but he saw me and jumped away, just in time, after I'd already pulled the trigger. Oh, God, Miss Lockett." Maggie covered her face with her hands. "It was an accident. I swear it. I was trying to *save* Danny, but I killed him instead."

Callie Mae stood frozen, her body heaving from the horror.

"It was how I found her," TJ added roughly. "Kneeling over Danny. By then, it was too late."

Callie Mae's throat burned. She couldn't think. Couldn't speak. Couldn't move from the pain.

Maggie lowered her hands. "My son took the blame for what I'd done, Miss Lockett," she said, tears streaming down her cheeks. "He was protecting me, that's all. Saving me from myself." She drew herself up to hold Callie Mae's gaze. "And all this time you've been hating him, you should've been hating me instead."

Chapter Thirteen

Emmett Ralston crept as close to their camp as he dared. Snatches of conversation drifted toward him, but one word in particular kept his senses on high-alert.

Danny.

He wedged himself between an outcropping of rock and some brush. Any closer, they'd see him for sure. But he had to hear, had to know what they were saying about the boy.

His stare latched on to Maggie Grier. She was doing most of the talking, and that was strange right there. In the short time he'd known her from back at Preston Farm, the woman never had much to say. When she did, she spoke real soft-like and didn't pay him much mind.

Which was fine with him, since he made it a point to keep to himself as much as possible. From the first day TJ hired him.

He had to.

But tonight, she was talking as if she had diarrhea

of the jawbone. Everyone stood around her, hanging on every word. And they looked as serious as ducks in the desert.

The Lockett woman, especially.

Emmett listened hard to learn more about what they found so fascinating about Danny-boy...and heard details about the night he died that no one else would know—the sequence of events that had happened so fast, so unexpected, they'd been a blur in his mind.

Until now.

The blur lifted like a cloud. Shock slammed into his belly like a fist.

Fighting to breathe, he gaped at the long gray braid, the slight build inside a man's denims, the baggy shirt...and realized the shrieking drunk who'd been hiding inside the C Bar C's horse barn that night...was *Maggie Grier?*

Beads of sweat dotted Emmett's brow.

He'd thought she was a man. God knew she fought like one. Things had happened fast, so damned fast— he hadn't taken the time to get a good look at her, not when his focus had been on Danny, to catch him before he got away...

A mistake, a mistake, a mistake.

The comprehension spun inside him. Left him nauseous from his own stupidity. If only he'd known, he would've killed her long before now to shut her up for good and keep TJ and Callie Mae Lockett from finding out.

Her stepfather, Penn McClure, too.

Now, everything made sense.

Emmett swiped a hand across his sweaty brow. And now, everything had changed.

TJ took the blame for what his crazy mother had done, but he'd want to get even for it. Revenge for Danny McClure. Emmett didn't know how much TJ knew. Wouldn't be long, he'd know too much, what with that agent he had working for him. And with Maggie Grier spilling her guts to everyone out there, hell, someone was bound to figure things out.

Emmett eased back from the brush. He had to go back to Kullen, let him know they had to get the hell out of Texas.

Fast.

If they didn't, they'd be dead.

Callie Mae sat at the stream's edge with her knees drawn up to her chest. A breeze blew over the water, chilling the late-night air, raising gooseflesh on her skin.

She hardly noticed. She stared out over the shimmering surface, cast to undulating shades of silver by the moon. Maggie's confession rippled through her mind, again and again, like the water incessantly lapping against the bank.

The woman's pain, her piercing heartache, had been real. Not once did Callie Mae think to question the truth of all she claimed. It made too much sense. Once the shock dissipated, the puzzle of inconsistencies of what Callie Mae believed—what they all believed—

about TJ's behavior fell into place and formed a clearer picture of the man he was.

Had always been.

An honorable one. A son strong enough to shoulder his mother's weaknesses. He loved her too much to allow her to suffer the ravages of a scandal, the scourges of interrogation by the law, being labeled a child-murderer by an unforgiving public.

He'd spared her all of it and showed no regret. Throughout his trial, he'd held his head high because he knew he'd done nothing wrong—except lie to save his mother. At the time of his trial, Callie Mae despised him for his arrogance. That appalling lack of remorse. She'd interpreted his pride as defiance of the law and being uncaring of the despicable act he'd done.

What she believed he'd done.

Callie Mae lowered her forehead to her knees and closed her eyes. She'd been quick to fall for his lie, though she should've recognized it as one. She'd known TJ almost her whole life. He'd grown into a man on the C Bar C, had shown his dedication to the ranch, her parents, *her,* untold times.

Too many times to count.

But the grief over losing her little brother had clouded reason, fueled the hate planted and nurtured by Kullen through flimsy evidence—

Kullen. She moaned aloud. What was his place in this? Why had he been so determined to dismiss TJ's claim that the shooting had been accidental? Why did he want TJ convicted? Had he latched too quickly on to TJ's confession and used it to glorify himself with an easy victory in the courtroom? A way to cinch himself a place in the C Bar C? Her legacy?

No, no. She moaned again in confusion. What was she thinking? Kullen would do nothing of the sort. As a shrewd lawyer, he had the means and ability to close the ugly chapter on Danny's death by enacting swift punishment on the man who claimed responsibility. Doing so had helped them heal, pick up the pieces and go on with their lives.

Except he was wrong.

They all were.

And now, what were they to do about it?

Behind her, a boot sole scuffed the grass and yanked her thoughts back to reality. She sat straighter with a jerk.

Wreathed in moonlight, TJ loomed over her. Dark and silent. Watching her.

What was he thinking? Did he hate her for believing the worst about him? Was he hurt beyond measure? Resentful that she didn't trust him?

"They're gone," he said finally.

Maggie, Boomer and Stinky Dale. Callie Mae hadn't told them goodbye. She should have. In light of the trouble they'd gone through, riding out here, concerned for their welfare and eager to help with Blue, well, it would've been the least she could do.

Now, the chance to speak with Maggie was gone. Delayed, at the very least, when an insufferable amount of time had already passed. After the woman's confession tonight, there'd been too much to grasp.

Too much to understand. With her head spinning, Callie Mae had rushed to the stream to be alone and sort it out.

No one had followed. They'd given her the privacy she needed and slipped away, headed for home, before she could notice.

Leaving her alone with the man convicted for killing her brother and who'd paid a higher price than he deserved.

"Now what, TJ?" she asked quietly.

"We get some sleep."

"That's not what I meant."

With the moonlight behind him, she couldn't see his expression. But she could feel the intensity of his gaze upon her. As if what he saw troubled him.

A moment passed. Then, he extended his hand.

For another moment, her glance lingered over its darkened shape, the long lean fingers, the broad palm. A hand that could gentle a newborn foal or break a bucking bronc. She'd learned how it could boldly caress a woman, too. Make her feel desired. Aroused. A hand that had always worked hard but…could never be capable of knowingly shooting a child.

Assured she wouldn't question that part of him again, she lifted her own, and he closed his fingers around hers to pull her gently, easily, to her feet.

She stood before him, the two of them in the moonlight. His fingers didn't let go, and neither did hers. Somehow, of their own accord, their fingers twined together. Their arms hung loose at their sides.

"I meant, where do we go from here?" she said.

"Nothing's changed, Callie Mae," he said. "We still need to find the truth from Kullen. First thing tomorrow, we'll head to Amarillo."

Hearing her intended's name tugged a frown between her brows and an unexpected ripple of dread. At seeing Kullen. At what he might say.

"When that's done," she persisted. "What then, TJ?"

Will you forgive me and simply go on with your life while I go on with mine? Or will you always despise me and those of us who hated you for what you'd said you'd done?

"Then I'm going to do whatever I can to keep you from marrying Kullen," he said.

His response startled her, and yet it shouldn't have. TJ had always made clear his contempt for the man. Callie Mae searched his shadowed expression.

"Why should it matter to you who I marry, TJ?" she asked, without accusation. Only curiosity.

"Everything about you has always mattered to me, Callie Mae," he rumbled. "Even when you were a kid."

She cocked her head, considering that. As her mother's favorite cowboy, TJ had been close to her parents. It was only natural, she supposed, he'd feel some responsibility toward her. He'd felt the same toward Danny. From the day her brother had been born.

"Most of the outfit did, I think," she said. "They've always been loyal to my family."

"Goes beyond loyal."

"Does it?"

"You should know it does."

Callie Mae didn't know what to think anymore. This confusion he brewed inside her. The way he turned her life upside down, when only yesterday she'd been straight-minded. In control.

"I love you, Callie Mae," he said quietly.

Her lashes lowered against an unexpected welling of tears. What had she done to deserve his devotion?

"Oh, TJ," she whispered.

With their hands still joined, he curled her arm behind her back and pulled her against him. Her forehead sank into his chest. Suddenly, everything about him filled her awareness—the faint scent of tobacco in the fabric of his shirt, the enticing combination of sweat and leather on his skin. His heat and strength, the hard breadth of his shoulders and chest...

His thumb stroked hers, and he slid his free hand into her hair, reminding her of how tangled the strands must feel to him. But he didn't seem to notice; instead, he coaxed her head back so she could look at him, and soon her vanity became lost in the feel of his rough palm against her cheek, the sensation of his strong thighs next to her slim ones.

Mostly, his lips hovering above hers.

Oh, the picture he made. A ruthless one with his cheeks rough and shadowed, his eyes heavily-lashed and black in the moonlight. As if he were a rugged desperado, bold enough to steal what he couldn't have.

Her knees weakened, and she feared they'd buckle

if she didn't hang on to him, and she slid her arm to his back and onto his shoulder, so she could.

"I want to make love to you, Callie Mae. Tonight," he said huskily.

She dragged in a breath and recognized the stirring of an ache his words created, deep inside her. "No. You can't. We mustn't."

He pulled her tighter against him, allowing her to feel the swollen length of his desire.

"You're the only one here to stop us," he murmured. "Is that what you really want to do?"

He was merciless in his persuasion, but she couldn't let him win. She struggled to hang on to reality.

"TJ, we have to talk about what your mother said tonight," she pleaded.

His head lowered; his jaw nuzzled her cheek, and her nerve endings sprang to life at the bristly feel of his beard, a sensation not unpleasant—

"She told you the truth." His breath swirled against her ear. "If you don't believe her, there's nothing more either of us can say or do to convince you about how Danny really died." Finally, his dark head lifted; his expression turned gravely serious. "Do you believe her?"

A vivid reenactment of the story Maggie told rolled through Callie Mae's mind. The poor woman had shed real tears; she'd endured an anguish no one with her fragile mental state could fake. She'd inspired horror and heartache in Callie Mae, as if little Danny had died all over again.

"Yes." Callie Mae nodded slowly. "I believe her."

Silent, he regarded her, as if to decide for himself if she meant it.

"What you did, TJ—"

"—had to be done."

No apologies. No explanations. His mother's would have to be enough. At least for now. His curt tone warned not to pursue the matter.

"Yes," she murmured, accepting it. "I suppose it did."

Still, she wondered how he survived the shame and those lonely days in jail. He'd lost everything he worked for. Stood for. The life he'd always known was gone—because he loved Maggie enough to throw it away.

He'd do the same for the woman who claimed his heart. Someone who would be his for the rest of her life.

A tiny sigh escaped Callie Mae. And how fortunate she would be.

Would Kullen be as gallant? As selfless?

With a certainty that left her increasingly troubled, Callie Mae thought not.

"Quit thinking so much," TJ commanded roughly.

His growled command cleared her mind with the realization his head was lowering, that his mouth waited over hers, enticing her all over again with a promise of what would come soon, very soon...

"How can I not?" she breathed, knowing she should step away, out of his embrace. She had no right to be here with him like this. Wanting.

She couldn't keep on wanting, but God help her, she did. She wanted him to kiss her like he did this morning, as if he were starved for the taste of her, an all-over kind of taste, demanding to be satisfied.

He groaned, low in his throat, and claimed her lips with a hunger that melted her bones into his. If she could've pressed herself closer, climbed into his skin and shared the heat of his blood, she would have. Her mouth opened. His tongue delved inward, hot and passionate, igniting a fire deep within her core.

He released the hand he held captive behind her back to hold her hard against him. His fingers splayed against her spine, as if to fill a need to touch as much of her as he could. She buried her hands in his hair, holding him to her, even as her mind protested that she couldn't keep on, couldn't keep on—

This passion TJ lit inside her was only sympathy for what he'd endured, she told herself. Or perhaps guilt, a plea for forgiveness for the hate she'd shown him, everyone had shown him, when he deserved none of it. And of course, she'd forgotten Kullen, to whom she was betrothed, and—oh, God, oh, God—what was she doing, kissing TJ instead?

"Stop," she whispered, her eyes closed during his seduction, her body absorbed in how he made her feel. "Stop, TJ."

His mouth dragged over her jaw, nuzzled into the curve of her neck. "Don't think of him, Callie Mae."

"I must." Forcing her head back, she pressed her fingers to TJ's lips. "Stop. Please."

Undeterred, he drew her fingertip into his mouth and suckled, his tongue deliciously warm and slick over her knuckle. She couldn't move away from this new sensation, the primal simplicity of it, if she tried.

Which she didn't.

"He's not entitled to your fidelity," TJ said and pressed a kiss into her palm. "One day, you'll see that."

"I've already betrayed him." Miserable, she eased her head onto TJ's shoulder, even as she despised her weakness in needing his comfort.

"I know you think of it that way, but—"

Her head came up. "If it was you, and the woman you planned to marry took her pleasure in another man's arms, wouldn't *you* feel betrayed?"

TJ frowned and brought her back down to his shoulder. "This is different."

"It's not."

He slid both hands down her torso, over the curve of her waist, then cupped her buttocks, kneading the flesh and bringing her full against him. His thick blade bulged through the front of his Levi's and left no doubt of his yearning. Why did he have this power over her? This appalling ability to keep her from ending these moments in his arms?

"Trust me, Callie Mae," he said, husky-toned. "That's all I ask."

"How can I when I no longer trust myself?" Dredging up every shred of willpower she possessed, she pushed out of his embrace, then took a step back. Two, for good measure. "Don't kiss me anymore, TJ. Do you hear me?"

His eyes narrowed. He nodded. Once. "I hear you."

"Promise me you won't."

A moment passed. "Not sure I want to, darlin'."

"Promise, or I'm saddling up and riding out of here right now. So you can't."

He took so long to respond, she began to fear she'd have to make good her threat. And she didn't want to leave. Not really.

"Guess you're starting to see your being with Kullen is wrong," he drawled. "Aren't you?"

"What's *wrong* is letting you love me up in his absence," she shot back.

TJ shifted and slid his fingers into his hip pockets. To keep from reaching for her again?

Finally, he shrugged. "All right, Callie Mae. I'll promise. If that's what you want."

She told herself it was. "Thank you."

His mouth formed a wry quirk. "You're welcome."

"Well, then." She tossed her head. "Good night."

Squaring her shoulders, she pivoted and headed back toward camp, leaving him staring after her.

And knowing it would be a long night.

For both of them.

Chapter Fourteen

"Kullen."

He dragged himself out of the blackest depths of sleep to comprehend the hushed sound. His name. Spoken from someone beside his hospital bed.

He cracked his eyes open. Hoped it was the good doctor or one of the young nuns who nursed him, ready to give him more of his precious morphine.

It wasn't. He opened his eyes wider, peered at the shape standing over him in his darkened room.

"It's me, Kullen. Emmett."

Seeing no one with him, Kullen twisted and scanned the room, to make sure. A dull pain shot through his thigh, a reminder of what Grier had done to him.

"Where's Callie Mae?" he demanded in a thick voice.

"She's still with Grier."

"What do you mean, 'she's still with Grier'?" he snapped.

"We got trouble, Kullen."

Emmett was prone to think calamity lurked around every corner. Nevertheless, if he didn't have Callie Mae with him, something must've gone wrong. Emmett rarely failed at what Kullen ordered him to do. Kullen pushed himself to a sitting position; he gnashed his teeth from the flare of fire in his leg.

Emmett moved away to quietly close the door, shutting out the faint light from the hall and keeping the sound of their voices from drifting toward the night nurses. He returned to fumble with the kerosene lamp on the bedside table and kept the flame low.

Kullen pondered the man's red-rimmed eyes, heavy-lidded from fatigue. From worry. He smelled of horse and dust; his clothes were wrinkled and dirty. Obviously, he'd ridden hard to get to Amarillo and St. Anthony's Hospital.

Kullen tried not to be alarmed. "What kind of trouble?"

"Maggie Grier was the one who shot McClure's boy. I heard her 'fess up tonight to Callie Mae."

Kullen stared. "TJ Grier's *mother?*"

Serious, Emmett nodded.

"But you said—" Kullen sputtered.

"I know what I said."

That a crazy drunk had come at him out of the shadows, struck him on the face with his whiskey bottle, chased after him with a shotgun...

From the way he—*she*, Kullen mentally corrected—had been dressed, they'd both assumed the attacker was male.

A mistake.

Then, the drunk had disappeared. Emmett had been stunned to hear TJ came forward, claiming guilt.

Kullen hadn't known what to think. His cousin's recollection wasn't normally faulty, but with no sign of the shadowed intruder, Kullen had been forced to change his strategy. He took advantage of Callie Mae and her family's grief to destroy TJ's reputation, feeding a gullible judge and jury lies to lock him in jail and neatly answer any questions about what happened to Danny.

The lack of evidence, however, had kept TJ's neck out of the hangman's noose. Still, his confession had fit into Kullen's plans so well, he'd all but forgotten about Danny's real killer.

Until now.

Damn, damn, damn.

"Who else was there with Grier's old lady?" he asked.

"Boomer Preston. And a friend of theirs, a cowboy named Stinky Dale."

Cooper. Stinky Dale Cooper. The unusual name dropped out of the past and into Kullen's brain like a stone.

Ten years ago in Dodge City, Stinky Dale had been one of the men from the C Bar C outfit who'd helped Penn McClure kill Rogan Webb. Callie Mae's father.

Several months earlier, McClure killed Bill Brockway, too. Kullen's father. In his determination to wreak revenge on McClure, Kullen had taken it upon himself to learn everything he could about his father's death. From the moment McClure shot Brockway in

Denver's Brown Palace Hotel, to that fateful day in Dodge City when McClure and several others from the C Bar C outfit set Rogan up for arrest.

Only he'd been killed instead.

Kullen had learned most everything that happened since then, too—with the exception of the true identity of Danny McClure's killer.

"Callie Mae took it hard, Kullen," Emmett said, sounding desperate. "Grier's old lady brought everything back and made it fresh again. Now, Callie Mae's going to want to know who it was in that barn tryin' to steal her brother. Just like Grier and everyone else."

Pain throbbed in Kullen's head. Right along with the throbbing in his thigh.

"They're going to find out about me, Kullen." Emmett swiped a hand across his mouth. "We have to hightail it out of here before they do."

Kullen had taken great care to cover his tracks in his quest to marry Callie Mae and surround himself with her money—of which every dime he deserved after what McClure had done. In his dreams to settle for a life of ease in Mexico, Emmett had been a willing accomplice.

Kullen refused to leave it all behind. A life of ease for himself, with Callie Mae's riches.

Still, Emmett was right about one thing. Lying in this damn hospital bed like an invalid made Kullen an easy target for TJ's vengeance—if he ever found out the truth.

Kullen flung aside the covers and braced himself for the ordeal ahead.

"Sure, Emmett," he lied. "Whatever you say."

His cousin would soon find out, however, he intended to take care of a few matters first.

"I'm cold, TJ."

Callie Mae's frustrated whisper tugged TJ awake. Night still shrouded their camp, but he figured it'd be dawn soon since he'd already spent too many hours remembering the feel of her in his arms and regretting that damned promise she'd forced him to make.

Not to kiss her again.

Only a heap of effort and an annoying sense of honor allowed him to keep the promise. Another heap of both kept him on his side, facing away from her, to keep him from being tempted.

And now she was cold?

Well, well, well.

Already, he began to feel better. He rolled over to check the fire and discovered it had dwindled down to a glow of embers, and yep, that chilled things, all right. Left the night air good and brisk. Not that he'd particularly noticed. He lowered his glance to Callie Mae and found her facing him, her blanket tucked to her neck.

"You're cold, eh?" he asked.

She nodded, and a shiver went through her. "I'm *freezing.*"

"Reckon I can help with that." He raised himself up on an elbow. "But then, that'd mean I'd have to put my arms around you to warm you up, and aw, hell, I already promised not to."

She frowned over at him. "TJ."

"I figure you're just likely to fight me on cozying up to you, being's I'm only a cowboy, and you're *the* Callie Mae Lockett who just happens to be engaged to—"

She clucked a shivery breath of exasperation. "TJ, stop."

"Then again, you did wake me up to complain, didn't you? Maybe I ought to just throw a few more pieces of wood on the fire and hope you get warm that way."

Her head lifted; her eyes slitted in a glare. "Are you going to invite me to share your blanket or am I going to have to force my way under it?"

Damned if her teeth weren't chattering.

Fighting a grin, he lifted one side of his wool covering, and she scurried under it, like a half-frozen mouse. After a few moments of combining bedrolls and adjusting blankets, she snuggled beside him with a kittenish purr.

"Better?" he murmured.

"Much. Oh, much." She peeped up at him from beneath her lashes. "Thank you."

"Why didn't you wake me sooner?" He rubbed her arm to warm her faster.

"I guess I was thinking too long on it."

Did she wonder if he'd refuse? He grunted. "What else were you thinking about?"

"If you're expecting me to say 'Kullen,' I wasn't." She frowned. "I should have been thinking about him, I suppose. But I wasn't."

He took some satisfaction from that. "What then?"

"I was thinking how I'll be glad to sleep in a real bed again. I want to wash my hair and take a long, hot bath." She wriggled a bit, as if to get more comfortable on the hard ground. "I wasn't born to sleep on the range."

Ceasing his arm-rubbing, his hand rested thoughtfully on her flat belly beneath the wool. "No."

She was destined for finer things. Luxury, power and comfort, all the advantages gained from her legacy. From her being a Lockett.

And yet she'd endured the rigors of chasing after Blue without complaint, her current chill excepted. She'd ridden and worked as hard as any woman could be expected. She'd been capable—and willing.

And too soon, he would have to let her go.

"How will this end, TJ?" she asked quietly.

Her question mirrored his thoughts, and she sounded as somber as he felt, which filled him with a sudden yearning to comfort her—hell, both of them—the only way he knew how. With his body. To make love to her then and there. Make time stand still and create a memory he'd be able to keep with him for a good long while.

It didn't matter that she'd promised herself to another. It had never mattered, and he leaned closer. His hand moved off her belly and over her ribs, his mouth craving her lips, his palm craving the feel of that supple globe of flesh hidden inside her shirt—

But her hand was faster, and she stopped him before he could satisfy either.

"We can't, TJ," she whispered. "Please. I don't know how much longer I can...keep telling you."

Her admission heated his blood. Assured him she didn't despise him as much as she used to. That she was weakening, and while that was a good thing, a very good thing, well, she was feeling a mite too vulnerable and he wanted her too much to take advantage of her that way.

His damned honor again, and he sighed. The day he claimed Callie Mae as his own was the day she came to him willingly, as hungry for him as he'd always be for her. Without a shred of resistance to hold her back.

Might be he was only dreaming it'd happen that way, but it was a dream he couldn't let go of. He eased away and pulled her closer. Her head settled on his shoulder, and for now, holding her, warming her, would have to be enough. He tugged her blanket higher to her neck.

"You didn't answer my question, Mr. Grier," she murmured after a moment.

He thought back to it, before his lust had taken over and distracted him. "About how this will all end?"

"Yes."

"It'll end with the truth."

She emitted a worried tsk. "Everything's such a mess, TJ. I'm scared what the truth will be."

He understood her fear. He'd lived through plenty of it himself over the past months.

"Better than not knowing," he said firmly. "The time's long past to right the wrongs that have been done to both of us."

"Of course." Her head moved in a quick nod. "Of course, you're right."

Despite her agreement, she still sounded apprehensive, and he dropped a reassuring kiss to her temple.

"Go to sleep, Callie Mae. Sun'll be up soon."

And with the arrival of dawn, the certainty of being unable to hold her any longer.

His chest tightened. Would he ever have another chance like this one?

Until she left him, he intended to savor the feel of her body snuggled against his, growing more relaxed the warmer she became.

Didn't take long for his imagination to kick in, thinking how her slim legs would feel entwined with his, without the cumbersome denim between them, the hard ground beneath, the air above chilly. To have the comforts of a real bed, a home of their own, a lifetime of nights together...

"TJ. Did you hear that?"

Callie Mae's whisper brought him instantly awake, and his senses hurtled into place. Brilliant sun dappled through the leaves, startling him with the realization dawn had long since arrived.

"Hear what?" he asked, his mind more on how he'd overslept than on her concern. Must've been the pleasure of having a beautiful woman against him, keeping them both toasty and sleeping as sound as babies.

"A horse, I think."

He took a few moments to listen, but heard nothing. His glance jumped toward their mounts, still hobbled.

"I think someone's coming," she said in a hushed voice.

He didn't take her concern lightly. "Stay put. I'll have a look around."

She drew back, giving him room to reach for Kullen's peashooter, stashed safely beside his bedroll.

A twig snapped.

TJ froze.

A crunch followed, not unlike an iron-shod hoof stepping over rocky ground, and TJ suddenly lunged for the pathetic-size Colt derringer while vehemently wishing for his shotgun which would've been a whole lot more deadly—

"Hold it right there, TJ, or we'll shoot."

He didn't move.

Callie Mae sucked in a breath of alarm.

They both twisted toward the three mounted men moseying into their camp, each with rifles cocked and leveled right at them.

TJ, in particular.

Woollie Morgan had been foreman for the C Bar C ranch for as long as TJ could remember. With him, Jesse Keller and Orlin Fahey, two of the most dedicated cowboys Carina and Penn McClure could have on their payroll.

And TJ had grown up right under their noses.

That they pointed weapons at him now rankled. Deep. A searing hurt rooted in his conviction for

Danny's death, years of friendship and camaraderie destroyed because of what TJ had done.

What Kullen had done.

Callie Mae flung aside the wool and scrambled to her feet.

"Put those rifles away. All of you," she ordered. "Woollie, what are you thinking, coming into our camp like this?"

None of them moved.

"I'm thinking I'm a mite disappointed you've let yourself be his blanket companion, teacup," Woollie said. "I wouldn't have expected it of you."

Her cheeks pinkened. "It wasn't like you think."

"I know what I saw."

TJ rose. "Nothing happened, Woollie. Not that it's any of your business if it had."

The foreman's eyes swung sharply toward him. His curly white beard being the reason for his nickname, the man had been a part of Callie Mae's life since the day she was born. When her own grandfather died a half-dozen years ago, Woollie had quietly stepped in to take his place, loving her as his own.

"Reckon she's a Lockett, TJ," Woollie said. "That makes her my business, all right."

"I've come to no harm with him." Chin kicked up, Callie Mae's voice rang firm.

The foreman grunted his skepticism. "Heard tell he put a gun to your head, young lady. That tells me right there he's put you in harm's way."

"He had his reasons."

"I'll bet he did."

TJ scowled in annoyance. Damned if Callie Mae was going to do his talking for him. "If you'd have been there, Woollie, you would've seen for yourself why things happened the way they did."

"Half the county's talking about what happened, TJ. I didn't have to be there."

Callie Mae set her hands on her slim hips. "Oh, Woollie, hush. I understand your concern, truly I do, but you can tell by looking at me, I'm just fine."

He skimmed her with a gaze—from the top of her uncombed head to her bootless feet—so thoroughly, she fidgeted. Pain darkened his eyes.

"Not sure I can tell that at all, honey," he said roughly, and shot TJ a condemning look.

"I am. I promise." Her voice had softened. Clearly, she read the concern in his gruffness. "Please don't worry."

He indicated her ill-fitting denims, the man's shirt. "What you're wearing isn't what it was when you left the ranch."

"No." In a self-conscious gesture, she stuffed the shirt hem more snuggly in the waistband of her Levi's, tidying herself for their perusal after a night of sleeping in her clothes. "I borrowed these from Stinky Dale Cooper. We stopped at his place for supper. How did you find us out here?"

Woollie lowered his rifle, as if convinced TJ wouldn't be a threat, after all. Jesse and Orlin followed suit. "When we heard about what happened, we rode out to the Coopers' place first. Figured they were nearest Preston Farm and might've seen you. Becky told us you were headed toward the Palo Duro."

"We were looking for TJ's horse."

"So I hear."

"We found him," TJ added, just in case any of them were interested.

Woollie said nothing. His silence stung, right along with Jesse and Orlin's. A year ago, the subject of TJ owning a racehorse as fine as Blue Whistler would've been fodder for a wagonload of interest from all of them.

Their lack of response only proved once again how much TJ had lost. Friends, who had once been like brothers to him.

"Reckon there's not much reason to stick around then, is there, Callie Mae?" Woollie asked. "Which horse is yours over there? We're taking you home."

"Not yet," TJ said, thinking of the truth he needed to find with her first.

"I have to ride into Amarillo to see Kullen," she added firmly.

The foreman shook his head, giving her another once-over, his expression indicating he didn't like what he saw. "You look like something the cat drug in, Callie Mae. Not fitting for a Lockett and for sure not fitting to be traipsing into a hospital. The way folks have been talking about you and what happened, you'll get 'em fired up even more." He jerked his chin toward the tethered horses. "I'm taking you home where it's safe."

"But—"

"No arguing."

"She's a grown woman, Woollie." TJ glowered. "Treat her like one."

"No, no, he's right, TJ." She tucked loose strands of hair behind her ear and stood a little taller, her feminine pride kicking in to change her mind. "I'll clean up before I ride in to see Kullen."

TJ sensed her pulling back from him, a shifting from the world they'd shared these past days to return to her own. A world where he didn't belong. He was losing her, too soon, and he wasn't ready.

"Callie Mae." He clenched his teeth, on the verge of embarrasing himself in front of the cowboys by begging her to stay.

As if she hadn't heard him speak, she turned back to Orlin. "My horse is the roan. Saddle him for me, will you?"

"Sure thing, Miss Lockett." Orlin slid his rifle into its scabbard and hefted his bulk out of the saddle. Paunch-bellied and balding, he moved with a grace one wouldn't expect for his girth. He avoided TJ's glance and set to work.

She strode toward the saddlebags to collect her things, but TJ snatched her wrist before she got there.

"Callie Mae," he grated. "I'll go with you—"

But even before he finished the sentence, he knew he wouldn't. Sadness filled her expression, and she shook her head.

"I'm sorry, TJ," she said quietly. "I don't think that would be wise."

Scalded by her refusal, he immediately released

her. Steeled himself against the truth of her words. The truth which would never be fair.

He gave her a cold smile. "It wouldn't, would it?"

She hesitated. "No."

She turned away. Before he knew it, she was saddled up and ready to ride, protectively flanked on either side by Woollie and Orlin. If she glanced at TJ, if she waved him a goodbye before they left, he didn't see it.

He refused to watch her leave.

Only the sound of hoofbeats told him she did.

Except, one of them held back.

Jesse.

And TJ braced himself to find out why.

Chapter Fifteen

"You always were crazy in love with her, weren't you, TJ?" Shaking his head, the cowboy sheathed his rifle.

TJ was in no mood for a confrontation. Jesse had worked at the C Bar C for a decade and a half; he'd been there from the very first day TJ joined the outfit, and TJ figured he could tell Jesse just about anything, including his feelings for Callie Mae.

Not anymore.

Jesse's allegiance would always be with Carina and Penn, and right now, that put him on the opposite side of the fence to TJ. Damn near made TJ bleed just thinking it, knowing it, but things being the way they were, it couldn't be helped.

"Best if you ride on out of here, Jesse," he said. "Else you'll never catch up with the other three."

"In due time. In due time."

Jesse swung a leg over the saddle horn and dropped

to the ground. Rooted in his shirt pocket. Pulled out a couple of quirleys.

He strode toward TJ, and TJ watched him come. That stride of his—lean, loose, bowlegged—and familiar. Like it'd been only yesterday since they'd cowboyed together on the C Bar C.

"Smoke?" Jesse asked.

"All right." TJ cleared his throat. "Thanks."

He remained wary. He couldn't figure why Jesse would stay behind when only minutes ago he'd leveled his rifle in TJ's direction.

Yet while they hunkered in the grass, both of them taking their first drags off their cigarettes, the silence between them turned…strangely companionable.

Just like old times.

"I never believed you, you know," Jesse said finally. "What you said about Danny."

TJ stilled. "That right?"

Jesse nodded, lifted a piece of tobacco off the tip of his tongue. "You were lying, weren't you?"

"About what?"

"Killing him."

"What makes you think I was?" TJ hedged, needing time to comprehend where Jesse was leading. How much he knew.

"No way you could've done it."

"Don't think so?"

"Nope." Jesse glanced over at him, then. Steady. Direct. "You were down in the valley, racing with the rest of us that night. We all saw you. No way you could've gone up to that horse barn in time to grab your shotgun and shoot him."

"I left early."

"Not early enough."

TJ stared straight ahead. Fought the ugly memories. Resisted the possibility Jesse might have figured out what Maggie had done and only despised TJ more for lying about it.

TJ had always made it a habit to check on Maggie. Still did, in fact. Every night. Just to make sure she was all right.

And that's what he'd done back then. Already half-drunk from the cold beer flowing freely among them, he left their racing early to check on Maggie. He'd been stunned to see the fire raging out of control, and he'd sobered up quick. Hearing the shotgun, finding that gut-wrenchingly small form crumpled in the dirt, his mother bent over and sobbing uncontrollably—

The horror and grief—sweet Jesus, he hoped neither of them had to live through anything like it again.

"You're coverin' for somebody, ain't you, TJ?"

TJ's throat worked. Tried to form a denial. Tell one more lie—

"You are. I know you are," Jesse said.

TJ could feel his piercing stare, as if the cowboy tried to delve into TJ's memories and see for himself what really happened that horrific night.

Despite Jesse's sharp perception, TJ couldn't trust him. Not yet. He hadn't seen the cowboy since the night Danny died. Why would Jesse speak up now, after all this time?

"Not going to talk about it, TJ?" he asked, his voice quiet, challenging.

"No."

"Suit yourself." He studied his cigarette. "We tried to help, though, just so you know."

"Help who?" TJ's head swung around. "Me?"

"Yep. Orlin, Ronnie Bennington, Billy Aspen. All of us, we went to see that lawyer Callie Mae's gone and hooked herself up with." Jesse took a puff off his stogie and exhaled. "Damn shyster."

"Kullen Brosius."

"Yeah, him."

"You did?" TJ couldn't hide his surprise.

"We tried to tell him you couldn't have done it because you were down in the valley with us, racing and drinking beer. We were all ready to swear to it, but he said without evidence, it was our word against the law's. Like he was bound and determined to see you convicted, didn't matter what we said. He threatened to have us arrested for harassing him and threw us out of his office after that."

Stunned, TJ could only stare.

"We would've come to the trial and spoke up for you, then, but we couldn't," Jesse continued. "Maybe you didn't know that, either."

"I didn't."

He recalled standing in front of the judge and feeling so damned alone, believing the outfit was too angry with him to bother to come. He'd been tortured from the hurt and contempt Callie Mae, Carina and Penn felt for him, too. He'd endured the trial without friends to assure him they'd be waiting when he got out of jail.

"Why didn't you come to the trial?" TJ hated asking, but he couldn't help himself.

"You didn't hear about the horses?"

TJ shook his head slowly. "What horses?"

Jesse heaved a long frustrated sigh, a frustration TJ was beginning to feel, too.

"After the new barn burned, we corralled the remuda down in the valley," the cowboy began. "The day of your trial, we woke up to find someone had kicked the pole fence in, and the herd had hightailed into the hills. We were roundin' 'em up for three days afterward."

"You think someone was trying to keep you out of the courtroom?"

"I'd bet my mama's bible on it."

"Hell, Jesse." TJ frowned.

"Now you know." Jesse ground out the cigarette into the dirt and rose. TJ rose with him. "If you need anything, just ask, y'hear?"

The offer moved him. "Appreciate it."

"I'd best be going." He mounted up. "One more thing, though."

"Yeah?"

"Don't let Woollie bother you none. Reckon he was as prody as a locoed steer this mornin', but he's always had a heap of respect for you." He pulled the brim of his hat lower onto his forehead. "Danny meant the world to him, that's all. So does Callie Mae and—"

"I know."

TJ had always known. And he understood. They were Woollie's family in a way that had nothing to do with blood.

"Good enough, then." Jesse touched a finger to his hat, turned his mount and rode off.

Back to the C Bar C.

Home.

If only TJ could go back, too.

A sharp dose of homesickness landed in the pit of his belly, right along with a new round of hate for what Kullen Brosius had done to him.

The newly built St. Anthony's Hospital and Sanitarium was a fine-looking, two-story brick building located in the northern part of Amarillo. In his haste to talk to Kullen, TJ didn't linger to marvel. He tied the buckskin to the hitching post and strode through the doors.

Once inside, however, his step slowed. The facility bustled with patients in wheelchairs and the good Sisters of Charity nuns garbed in their navy-blue habits and starched white wimples. An abundance of windows filled the area with light, but there seemed to be a somber mood about the place.

Maybe it was only the hushed voices and serious expressions on the Sisters, but the feeling was palpable.

TJ shook the mood off. His concern lay only with finding Kullen's room and pulling the truth out of the man's conniving throat.

He approached an elderly, small-boned woman seated behind a large desk. She made notations in a ledger and appeared absorbed with her work, but noticing TJ in front of her, she gasped in surprise and pressed a blue-veined hand to her breast. Her wide-eyed glance dropped over him, then lifted quickly. She paled.

"Pardon me." Aware of how he must look after two days on a horse, TJ removed his Stetson and raked his fingers through his hair. He found a smile to assure her. "I'm looking for someone."

"Oh, forgive me." Her hand lowered, and faint color infused her thin cheeks again. "You gave me a fright."

Might be he looked worse than he thought; he should've taken the time to shave and clean up before coming. Or maybe the poor thing just tended to be easily nettled.

"Sorry," he said. "Didn't mean to."

"We've had a dreadful morning, and it isn't even noon yet. I'm a bit jumpy, I'm afraid." She shook her head sadly and closed the ledger. "You say you're looking for someone?"

"Yes."

She reached for a black-bound book emblazoned with St. Anthony's Hospital Registry. "What was the name of this someone?"

"Kullen Brosius."

Again, her cheeks paled. "Brosius!"

"That's right," he said, uneasy from her reaction.

"He's not here, TJ."

TJ swung around toward the gruff voice behind him. Paunch-bellied Sheriff Dunbar stepped out of one of the patient rooms with his jaw set grim. A white-haired gentleman, dressed in a dark suit and appearing equally somber, followed him.

"Sheriff." TJ nodded a stiff greeting and put his hat back on. He hadn't seen the lawman since Dunbar took him to jail last year. Was his stern tone a forewarning he still held a grudge against TJ?

The question had no sooner formed in his thoughts than the sheriff's words clicked in his brain.

"What do you mean, 'he's gone'?" TJ demanded.

"They found him missing a few hours ago." Dunbar halted in front of him.

Shocked rolled through TJ. "He was wounded—"

"So I hear."

Questions pounded against his temples, but TJ held them back, expecting the lawman to chastise him for being responsible for shooting Kullen. Never mind it was self-defense…

"Sounds like he had it comin'," Dunbar said, his gray-eyed perusal shrewd.

"He did." At least they agreed on that part of the matter. TJ regarded him back. Like one enemy testing the other. "How'd you know?"

"Boomer Preston stopped by my office a couple of days ago and informed my deputy. Seemed Boomer came to town because he needed medical attention, too. Unfortunately, I was gone to Dallas with the missus, so Boomer reported to the deputy what happened out at his farm. He said Brosius would've killed you if he could."

"He would've."

"I came over to investigate. Among other things."

Except the lawman was too late. They both were.

TJ fought frustration. "What other things?"

"Excuse me."

TJ glanced over at the older man, standing slightly behind Dunbar and blatantly eavesdropping. TJ had all but forgotten he was there.

"I'm Dr. Feldman," the gentleman said, and he held out his hand.

TJ clasped it firmly. "TJ Grier. I put the bullet in Kullen's leg."

"I was his surgeon." He stood back, threaded his fingers behind his back. "His injury was quite complicated, I'm afraid. Mr. Brosius wouldn't be able to leave this hospital without a great deal of pain and assistance."

"I have an idea who helped him," TJ said.

"Let me guess." Dunbar reached into his pocket and pulled out a small pad, scribbled with notes. "Emmett Ralston."

"That's right." TJ gave him a cold smile.

"Boomer reported what he knew about the man." The sheriff returned the pad to his pocket. "You think they're in cahoots with another?"

"I know so."

"Perhaps we should investigate the plausibility of

Mr. Ralston also being responsible for the thievery of our pharmaceuticals," Dr. Feldman suggested sadly.

TJ's glance sharpened. "What happened?"

The sheriff heaved a sigh. "Sometime before dawn, someone broke into the hospital's pharmacy and stole a quantity of morphine vials."

"If that weren't enough, he gave poor Sister Carlotta the scare of her life." The elderly lady at the desk sniffed, listening in behind them. "We were all terrified for her."

"Sister was on duty when the attack occurred," Feldman explained. "She was Mr. Brosius's nurse, I might add, and we all admired her skills and compassion. That she was treated so roughly was unforgivable."

"He clunked her on the head but good. Knocked her cold," Dunbar added. "One of the other nuns found her tied up with her rosary in a cleaning closet."

"Is she all right?" TJ asked.

"Doing better." Feldman indicated the room he'd just vacated with the sheriff. "I'm afraid I had to sedate her, and she's sleeping soundly for the time being. I suppose her injuries could have been worse."

"Did she get a look at her attacker?" TJ had to know.

"Only that he had a beard."

Fury building, TJ locked gazes with the lawman. "Emmett Ralston."

"I guessed as much," he said. "Don't suppose you know where they would've gone?"

"If I knew, I'd go after them," TJ growled.

Their gazes didn't waver.

"Reckon you would at that, TJ," Dunbar said quietly.

Doctor Feldman straightened. "I certainly hope both of them are apprehended as soon as possible. I'll leave you to your work, Sheriff. I have patients to attend to." He inclined his head toward TJ. "Good luck to both of you."

After he left, TJ had no further reason to stay.

But he was strangely reluctant to leave.

Sheriff Dunbar had been a friend long before TJ's troubles started over Danny. Fair and even-tempered, his consistent reelections to his post proved he was well-liked and trusted throughout the county.

Dunbar never believed TJ's lie about killing Danny. He'd made that plain throughout his interrogation, but TJ hadn't budged from his story. It pained the lawman deeply to throw TJ into his jail until sentencing, then deport him to the state penitentiary in Huntsville shortly thereafter. TJ had seen it etched on the sheriff's grizzled face, but he'd been bound to obey the judge's decree, and obey the decree, he did.

"How are you, TJ?" Dunbar asked quietly.

The events of the past days paraded through his mind. The altercation with Kullen. The scare of losing Blue, then finding him. His time with Callie Mae, especially. The memory of holding her in his arms, tasting her lips. Wanting her, more than he'd ever wanted her before.

He tamped down the memories. The ache that never seemed to go away. "Well enough."

"Good to see you."

"Better than the last time, anyway." Rueful, TJ quirked his mouth.

"Reckon that's behind us now. Thank the Almighty." Dunbar shook his head in regret. "But now this happened. Suppose Callie Mae is at her ranch?"

"That's where she was headed."

"Then I'm going to ride on out and tell her that her intended is missing. She'd want to know."

Unfortunately, she would.

The knowledge fouled TJ's mood.

"Kullen won't give her up easily," he said. "We have to assume he'll head out to see her at some point."

"I'll make sure the stagecoach and railroad stations keep an eye out in case he tries to leave town, though," Sheriff Dunbar said, heading for his horse. "I have a few questions I'm figurin' he'll have answers for."

"Makes two of us."

The lawman paused. "Let me do my job, TJ. Stay out of this." His warning rang firm. "They tried to kill you once, and mark my word, they'll try again."

TJ didn't respond and swung onto the buckskin. He might never find the truth if he had to depend on someone else to do it for him.

For now, however, Callie Mae was safe. Woollie would make sure she was, and that gave TJ some comfort. Fact was, TJ had Blue to think of, too. For now, he'd ride out to Boomer's and make sure everyone there was all right.

Then, he'd find a way to see Callie Mae again.

Any way he could.

Chapter Sixteen

Later that night, Callie Mae stood at her bedroom window staring out into the shadowed ranch yard. The moon shone like a glowing ball pasted against the black, star-studded sky. The night was calm, eerily still. Not a leaf moved on the trees.

She didn't know the hour, but she didn't care enough to find out from the clock on her bedside table. Midnight, perhaps. Maybe later.

It didn't matter.

Only the decision she had to make did.

What was she to do about Kullen?

Sheriff Dunbar's visit early this afternoon had thrown the ranch into a tailspin. Kullen's escape from the hospital shot suspicion through the outfit which proved catching. Why would he risk further injuring himself by abandoning the care and recuperation he very much needed?

Because he had something to hide?

The fact that vials of morphine were stolen from St. Anthony's pharmacy fit the picture of a man desperate to flee his crimes. That Emmett Ralston might've helped him did, too. It would've been almost impossible for Kullen to escape by himself, given his invalid condition. He would've needed Emmett's help.

Were they guilty of wanting to harm Danny, as TJ insisted?

If so, *why?*

And TJ. Oh, God. She couldn't shake him from her thoughts. He'd branded himself onto her heart. A brand she had no right to allow.

But she had.

She'd betrayed Kullen in a way far different than he likely betrayed her, but one equally unforgivable. And unexpected. She'd been so sure Kullen would make the perfect husband, the best match for her beloved Lockett legacy.

Had she made a terrible mistake?

She feared she had.

These past days with TJ had taught Callie Mae awareness for a man like she'd never had with Kullen. An earthy, muscle-and-bone kind of awareness. TJ was at one with the land, with sweat and horses and hard work. He needed self-respect and honor in every fiber of his being to be able to look himself in the mirror each morning. A man capable of immense love so deep, so powerful, a woman would always know she had his complete and undivided devotion.

How fortunate she would be.

Callie Mae remembered how TJ had declared his feelings for her. Without hesitation. But was it born of lust? The immediacy of their situation? Their being alone, working together to find his horse?

Perhaps.

Yet Kullen claimed to love her, too. Did he have an eye toward power? Money? Glory?

The C Bar C could give him all those things.

Why hadn't Callie Mae seen it before?

Still, maybe she was wrong. Maybe everyone—TJ, Sheriff Dunbar, Woollie and the rest of the outfit—was merely overreacting to his behavior. Maybe his reasons for escaping St. Anthony's hospital meant something different, something completely logical.

Then again, maybe it didn't.

Nothing made sense.

Concerned that Kullen might try to contact her, or even retaliate against her, Woollie and the sheriff assigned C Bar C men to take turns guarding the house. Her. She'd protested, loudly, that Kullen would never hurt her.

But they hadn't listened, and Callie Mae could see armed cowboys right outside her bedroom window.

They made her feel like a princess in an ivory tower. Come morning, she'd put a stop to this ridiculous over-protectiveness. She could take care of herself with Kullen. She'd planned to marry him, for pity's sake.

Movement in the yard distracted her thoughts, and she recognized Jesse Keller taking Orlin Fahey's place as guard. Their indiscernible voices drifted upward through her half-open window; soon, the older man's darkened shape shuffled off in the direction of the bunkhouse, and the yard fell silent once again.

Mentally drained, her bed finally beckoning, Callie Mae turned away. After removing her robe and tossing it over a chair, she pulled back the quilts on the big four-poster and climbed beneath. Her body settled into the pillow and mattress; the crisp sheets felt cool, heavenly…

A sound brought her instantly awake.

Callie Mae's gaze darted toward the open window; a light breeze played with the hems of the curtains. Moonlight spilled inward, bringing with it…silence.

She didn't move. Didn't breathe. Yet she sensed something wasn't right.

Her heart pounded. Suddenly, behind her, the mattress dipped. A hand clamped over her mouth. Locked the scream in her throat.

"Don't be afraid, Callie Mae."

She stilled at the low whisper, gently spoken. Husky. Familiar.

The hand eased off her mouth. Her head swiveled on the pillow. A dark, rugged face loomed over her, and her eyes widened in recognition.

"TJ!" she gasped.

He held a finger to his lips. "Shh."

"What are you—"

"Shh, darlin'."

She rolled to her back. "Don't 'darlin'' me," she

hissed, though she took care to make it a quiet hiss. "What are you *doing* in here?"

For a moment, his gaze lingered over her face. The shadows sharpened the angles of his jaw, his chin, making him appear ruthless and dangerous.

Wildly exciting.

He reached out and tenderly threaded his fingers through her hair.

"I couldn't stay away," he said.

The words sounded wrenched from him. Her heart tilted and swayed. "You should have."

"I know."

She darted a quick look at the closed door. "Woollie will have a fit if he finds—"

"I know that, too."

"TJ." She bit her lip. The mattress dipped again. He shifted his position and swung his body around to straddle hers. She pushed on his hard thighs. "TJ, you can't be in here."

"No other place I want to be." He planted his hands near her shoulders, lowered his head and nuzzled her neck. "Don't send me away, Callie."

She fought to breathe, to think. Fought for strength to resist him, but dear God, already her bones were melting from having him with her like this, her blood stirring from a slow fire.

"TJ." Her lashes drifted closed. His scent assailed her—shaving soap, wind and leather. "How did you get in here?"

Her room was located on the second floor. Woollie

set up a cot in the parlor, protecting her from inside the house while her parents were gone. It would've been impossible for TJ to slip past him. Impossible.

"Jesse was willing to do me a favor." His smooth jaw rubbed against hers; he grazed her chin with his teeth. "And that big ol' tree outside your window has some mighty strong branches."

Her eyes flew open in alarm; her glance jumped toward the fluttering curtains on the adjoining wall.

"You crawled in through the *window?*"

He chuckled softly. "Like I said. I couldn't stay away."

His breath mingled with hers. The bulk of his body filled her vision and hid the moonlight. Somehow, her hands had found their way from his thighs into the thickness of his hair.

"Oh, TJ."

"Let me stay with you tonight." He turned serious, the low timbre of his voice rough. Insistent.

"You can't. We mustn't." Her lashes drifted closed again. She couldn't help it, not with the way his tongue traced the shape of her mouth, igniting an ache to be kissed. Again and again. "TJ, this is crazy."

Never had she had a man in her bed. But then, never had she slept with one, either. Not until TJ, the two of them together these past nights.

Only him...

"What's crazy, Callie Mae? Wanting you like this? Not being able to get you out of my mind?"

"Yes." He'd yet to ease his teasing assault, and she

arched a little to meet his lips, to satisfy this growing need to be ravaged…

But he drew back some, so she couldn't.

"I've wanted you for so long, it feels like my whole life," he murmured. "Seems like I need to make love to you, just to get you out of my system."

"Kiss me, TJ."

"Believe me. I want to."

Again his head lowered, this time for her earlobe, tantalizing nibbles that sent her nerve endings sizzling.

"Why don't you then?"

Like the pathetic wanton she seemed to be, she turned her face into him, rooting for his kiss like a suckling babe at the breast.

"'Cuz I promised not to."

"When?"

"Yesterday. You made me."

"I made you promise not to kiss me?" For the life of her, she couldn't remember. Not when she wanted him to kiss her now. A mindless kind of wanting. "I didn't."

"You did. And I'm a man of my word."

"I'll understand if you break it this time."

His dark head lifted. If she expected him to be amused, he wasn't.

"Up to now, Callie Mae, I've let you call the shots. But from here on out, we play by my rules. If I kiss you, I'm not going to stop at one. Or two. Or three."

He paused, as if to allow her time to comprehend the immensity of what he said. And wanted. The depth of his desire for her. That they both hovered at the point of no return.

"When I start, I won't stop," he continued huskily. "It's all or nothing for us, darlin'. All or nothing."

And she understood. If she refused him, it'd be the end. He would leave, and she might never see him again.

Is that what she truly wanted?

"I love you, Callie Mae." He trailed his knuckle over her lips. "No matter what, I'll always love you."

Emotion welled in her throat. They were words he wouldn't give away lightly to anyone. This proud and honorable cowboy who loved everything about her— her home, her land, the woman she'd become.

"I can't send you away this time, TJ," she said, her voice whisper-soft. "God help me, it's too late for that."

For a moment, he didn't move.

Then, he drew back. Eased off the bed. And began to unbutton his shirt. By the time he removed his denims and boots and left them all in a pile on the floor, the blood hummed in her veins with anticipation.

He stood over her, silhouetted in the moonlight. A perfect vision of lean masculinity. Of contoured muscle. And unabashed desire.

Callie Mae wanted him—in ways that went beyond the pleasures a man and woman would share together. Ways too complicated to comprehend at the moment, but something her instincts unavoidably insisted.

She would figure it all out later.

Much later.

But for now, she watched him bend toward her and

fling aside the quilts. His hands bold and sure, he slid his palms up her legs, from her ankles to her knees, his work-roughened skin deliciously warm and sensual against hers. When he grasped the hem of her night-gown along the way up, she lifted her hips, then her arms, and in moments, the filmy garment drifted downward and landed atop his boots.

TJ drank in the sight of her.

"You're beautiful, Callie Mae," he whispered. "As beautiful as I knew you'd be."

She trembled. He spoke with such reverence…an unquestioned yearning. Wordlessly, without shy-ness, she reached for him, and then he was there, in her arms, rolling with her on the bed, bringing her on top of him, murmuring her name, again and again.

Their mouths met, at last, in an uncontrolled burst of hunger. Wet and frenzied, their tongues swirled and curled, igniting the fires of passion, making them burn higher, hotter, turning their breathing ragged and rough.

"I can't get enough of you, Callie Mae."

TJ's voice rasped with the admission, and his hands lowered to her hips. He lifted her, and she grasped his shoulders, holding herself above him while he took one nipple into his mouth and suckled the sensitive nub with his tongue. She gasped at this new sensation. Her muscles turned to jelly. She feared she'd collapse into a boneless heap if he wasn't there to keep her from it.

"O-oh, TJ," she moaned.

He did the same with the other side; her head fell

forward, her hair a silken veil around them, her body awash in glorious sensation that built inside her, deep within her feminine core, higher and higher.

His velvet blade throbbed against the inside of her thigh. She needed more from him, an ending to this sweet torture, and she fitted herself over him.

"Callie. God, Callie." TJ groaned and thrust himself inside her, a deliciously slick sheathing that had her gasping yet again in newfound revelry.

He filled her, connected with her in the perfect way a man was meant to fill a woman. Yet she ached for still more, and her hips began to rock. She found the rhythm, seeking the completion that begged to be reached. TJ clasped her hips, keeping her tight against him, and he rocked with her. Faster, harder. Frenzied. Over and over until they fell into that glorious abyss together and shattered into a million pieces.

Blissfully satisfied.

"Why do you call your mother 'Maggie'?" Callie Mae asked.

She laid with her legs entwined with TJ's, her head on his broad shoulder. Far from sleepy, she toyed with the dark crisp hairs sprinkled across his chest, lazily twirling them around her fingertip.

He stroked her arm, long and unhurried caresses that showed he'd yet to sate his need to touch her.

"Because that's what everybody else called her, I suppose," he said.

"She never wanted you to say 'mama' or 'mother'?"

"Not that I recall. For as long as I can remember, she's always been just 'Maggie.'"

"Hmm." Callie Mae found it strange, but she refrained from saying so.

"She never saw herself as a good mother, even when I was very young." His voice grew quietly pensive. "She moved around a lot, depending on which man she was living with at the time. My grandmother had to take me in."

"What about your father?"

"What father?" Callie Mae felt his mouth turn into a sarcastic quirk against her temple. "I don't think she ever knew for sure who he was."

"Oh." She sighed, at a loss for words. "I'm sorry, TJ."

"Don't be. It doesn't matter anymore." His arm tightened in a quick, reassuring squeeze. "When my grandmother died, Maggie had to learn how to raise me. There was no one else. But her drinking made it impossible most days. I learned how to take care of her instead."

She stroked his chest. "You grew up fast then, didn't you?"

He shrugged. "I was barely fifteen when I came to the C Bar C."

She remembered he'd been devoted to the ranch even then, starting as a wrangler and growing into one of the best cowboys the C Bar C ever had.

"But for all her faults, Callie Mae, she would never have knowingly hurt anyone. Including Danny."

Callie Mae tilted her head back and kissed him. "I believe you."

"And not once, I swear, has she had a drink since then. I would've known if she had."

She kissed him again. "I believe you on that, too."

"What she went through, what she'd done, cured her from ever getting drunk again."

"TJ." Callie Mae laid her fingers gently against his mouth. "You don't have to defend her to me anymore. Are you worried I hate her?"

His expression turned pained, and he pressed his lips to her palm. "Yes."

"I don't. Now that I know her side of it, well—"

Callie Mae halted. In her weakness and grief, she'd found it easier to seek refuge in hate, but now, could she forgive?

"I guess I understand," she continued slowly. "I intend to tell her so, when I see her next."

A moment passed. She sensed he struggled with an emotion he was reluctant to let her see.

"I love you, Callie Mae," he said roughly, but he eased her onto her back with gentleness. "And because I love you—" he spread her thighs with his knees "—I'm going to show you—" his head lowered "—just how much."

His tongue found her innermost petals of femininity, stroked and worshipped and swept her away on tidal waves of sensation, making her realize, in the tiniest corner of her mind, that not once since TJ had crawled into her bed had she thought of Kullen.

And now, it was too late.

Chapter Seventeen

A firm knocking sound tugged TJ out of pure contentment and threw him into the startling reality of morning. Warned him that sun beamed in through the open windows. That it was late. That Callie Mae lay in his arms with her sweet fanny snuggled warmly against his naked groin.

Another knock sounded. "Callie Mae? Are you up yet?"

His brain worked to identify the muffled voice on the other side of the door. Female...

Callie Mae started awake.

"Callie!" The voice called again.

Her head lifted off the pillow. Her gaze shot across the room in absolute mortification.

"Oh, no!" she whispered hoarsely. "My mother!"

Surprised, he rose up on an elbow and remembered to keep his voice low. "She's back already?"

"Can I come in?" Carina called.

"No!" Callie Mae sat up and clutched the sheet against her breasts with one hand, raked her rich cinnamon hair back from her face with the other. "I—I'm getting dressed, Mother. What are you doing home so soon?"

"Meet us downstairs for breakfast, and I'll explain. Can you hurry?"

"All right." Callie sat frozen, her eyes on the door.

Footsteps headed down the stairs and faded away.

Callie Mae blew out a breath, fell back against the pillow and turned her panicked blue gaze on him. "She'll *kill* me if she finds out you're here."

He regarded her. "You're not going to tell her?"

She didn't move. "I don't think so."

He caressed her cheek. "Regrets, darlin'?"

"I'm not sure yet." Her delectable lips turned downward.

"Want me to leave?" He jerked his chin toward the window he'd climbed through earlier. "Like a schoolboy caught with his pants down?"

He wavered between anger that she didn't see their time together like he did—and knowing the predicament he'd put her in.

"TJ, try to understand." She trailed her fingers down his arm, her expression beseeching. "It's complicated between us."

"Only if you let it be." Tersely, he flung back the covers and strode toward her side of the bed, to his clothes still in a heap on the floor. He grabbed his Levi's.

"What are you going to do?" she asked, laying there

clutching the sheet and looking so damned beautiful with her hair tousled, her lips full and her skin rosy. Like she'd spent half the night making love.

Which she had.

"Go downstairs," he said. "The normal way."

"TJ." She sat up again and drew her knees to her chest.

"I figure there's a few things your parents need to know." Finished buttoning his pants, he reached for his shirt next. "My bedding you being only one of them."

"TJ, listen."

"If it's any consolation, I'll pave the way. By the time you come down, they'll already know I spent the night with you." He tossed her a cold smile.

"I don't expect you to fight my battles for me."

"Is that what I'm doing?" He stuffed his shirt hem into his waistband.

"They'll think I betrayed Kullen and—"

"He betrayed you first, Callie Mae. Months ago."

"Even so, my behavior with you was unacceptable under the circumstances."

"We're adults." Pulling on one boot, he reached for the second. "We both knew what we were doing. And I don't recall you pushing me away."

"I didn't. I know I didn't." She looked so miserable, his heart squeezed. "I wish everything would stay like it was last night forever."

His annoyance vanished at her pouty admission, and he bent toward her with a throaty groan, cupped the back of her head and helped himself to the sweetness of her lips. Her arms circled his neck, and the sheet dropped to her lap. TJ filled his palm with the weight of one breast and savored a leisurely fondle.

"Me, too," he whispered, ending the kiss. He straightened and strode to the dresser to borrow her hairbrush; he gave his hair a quick run-through, though there wasn't much he could do about his unshaven cheeks. She wouldn't have a razor or shaving soap. He braced himself for the confrontation ahead. "Don't be long."

She yanked up the sheet, covering herself just before he opened the door. Her chin lifted, as if she braced herself, as well. "I'll be there."

Little had changed in the house since TJ had been inside last. Same dark varnished floors. Same thick rugs. Same heavy furniture. He even remembered how the third step tended to creak when someone stepped on it just right.

Like now, when he did.

The dining room's wide, open doorway faced the stairwell, and at the creaking sound, heads lifted. Expecting their surprise that it wasn't Callie Mae, TJ descended the last step and strode into the room.

He wasn't disappointed.

Still a beautiful woman with her hair a deep brunette shade, her eyes that intriguing color of indigo, Carina Lockett McClure sat next to her husband with an authority deserving of a cattle queen. Seeing TJ, she stopped stirring milk into her coffee and slid a sharp glance up the stairs, then swung her gaze back to him. And paled.

Penn breathed an oath.

But it was Woollie who made the most noise, dropping his fork with a clatter against the plate and emitting a strangled sound of shock.

"Where the *hell* did you come from?" he choked.

"Reckon it's clear where he came from," Penn said, easing back in his chair, though his leather-brown eyes remained darkly riveted on TJ.

"Tell me it wasn't my daughter's bedroom," Carina said coolly, resuming her stirring.

TJ halted. "Can't do that, Carina."

She continued stirring. Except for the tightening of her fingers on the spoon, she held her emotion in check. "Then at least tell me you didn't hurt her."

Her worry that he would stung deep. He waited for the unpleasant sensation to pass. "She's always meant a hell of a lot to me."

"So you've said." Carina set the spoon down, lifted the china cup and sipped. "She was agreeable to your… visit?"

A rush of just how agreeable she'd been swarmed through him, sweet as molasses.

"Yes," he said simply.

"I see."

At a rare loss for words, she turned to Penn. He reached out, took her hand into his and returned his attention to TJ.

TJ could feel the subtle shift in command. Seemed

motherhood threw Carina into tumult, and she needed Penn to handle matters for a spell.

The man was capable. Often like a big brother to TJ, other times a revered boss, and still others like an adored father, Penn McClure had firmly staked his place as head of the C Bar C alongside Carina. Untold hours in the sun had tanned his skin and lined his face in a manner most found appealing. With his hair only slightly peppered with gray, he remained a handsome man, lean and fit, and still fiercely in love with his wife.

"Sit down, TJ." Penn indicated covered dishes on the table. "Flapjacks. Bacon. Scrambled eggs. Help yourself if you're hungry."

The offer startled him; TJ stayed careful. "Can't say as I expect your hospitality, Penn. Considering."

Penn's grim nod indicated he understood what TJ meant. The last time they spoke, the conversation had been far from friendly.

"Reckon all that's in the past now, isn't it?" Penn said.

TJ couldn't begin to think what brought on the man's forgiveness, but if he was offering the proverbial olive branch, TJ was inclined to accept it. To say he missed Penn's friendship was an understatement.

Besides, no one attempted to throw him out of the house or burn some powder on him. Another good sign. Even with Woollie watching him with unguarded suspicion, TJ was compelled to accept Penn's invitation.

The room had fallen as silent as a fence post, but he sat. Instinct told him they were waiting for him to explain his being with Callie Mae, but he figured it best to give them time to get used to him first. So he filled his plate and shoveled a forkful of eggs into his mouth.

Finally, Woollie tapped the coffeepot with his butter knife. "It's hot if you want some."

TJ nodded with equal curtness. "I do. Thanks."

He reached for the pot. The front door opened, and footsteps trod across the carpet. Grew louder in their approach. A man wearing a gray suit appeared in the wide doorway, a file of papers in one hand, as if he'd just gone outside to retrieve them, and TJ nearly poured black brew on Carina's starched tablecloth.

"TJ!" Harvey Whelan, all the way from Washington, D.C., stopped short. "Why, I didn't know you'd be here."

"I'll say the same about you," TJ growled.

He plunked the coffeepot down. The hatless and balding United States Treasury agent reached over and shook his hand with an apologetic grimace.

"I'm sure you find my presence quite puzzling," he said.

TJ refrained from swearing. He'd been on pins and needles for weeks waiting to hear from the man. And he came to the C Bar C *first?* "You could say that."

TJ's mind raced. Harvey knew something. Something important, and sweet Jesus, it had to be about Danny.

The truth TJ craved.

The facts Penn and Carina needed to hear.

"I assure you, I was going to ride straight to Preston Farm next." The government agent laid his file on the table and settled himself in his chair. Only then did TJ notice the half-finished meal on the plate. The unfolded napkin, set aside. The empty coffee cup. Clearly, the man had pulled in early enough to join Penn and Carina for breakfast. "But of course, this is more opportune."

Ten years ago, Harvey had been instrumental in helping Penn arrest Callie Mae's unscrupulous father, Rogan Webb, in a counterfeit ring case in Dodge City. Rogan Webb ended up dead, and Harvey had been a loyal friend of Penn and Carina's ever since. His experience, trustworthiness and access to important investigative files proved him a true asset. TJ couldn't think of a better man to help him clear his name.

"You may as well know, TJ, we no longer believe you shot Danny," Carina said quietly, as if she could read his thoughts.

TJ's attention jumped to her. He didn't move.

"Wasn't like you, even if you claimed it was an accident," Penn concurred. "We knew how much our son meant to you. You'd made it as plain as the horn on your saddle often enough."

"You were covering for someone, weren't you?" Carina spoke in her cool, authoritative voice, the one that said she was convinced of what she said.

TJ's brain digested the news and battled the merits of protecting Maggie, one more time…or getting the whole damn thing off his chest. For good.

"Imagine our surprise when Harvey informed us you'd requested his services." Penn regarded TJ with an inscrutable expression.

"Guess you needed to find out what happened that

night, too." Woollie, watching him, bit off a piece of crispy bacon.

TJ cleared his throat, swept his glance over the four of them. "There was someone else in the horse barn. I need to find out who it was and why he was there."

Harvey clasped his fingers. "Under the circumstances, I kept TJ's request for my help in the strictest confidence until the last possible moment, but based on my investigation of what happened the night Danny was killed, I have reason to believe Callie Mae is in danger. Which is why I rode out here to the C Bar C first."

TJ's belly clenched. "You have evidence?"

"Not quite. But close. I've uncovered crucial information which explains motive," he said grimly.

A stair creaked then, and TJ's glance lifted to the stairwell. To Callie Mae walking down, one step at a time with her head held high, her hand on the polished banister, as if she needed the thing for support. To give her the courage she needed to face them in light of what she and TJ had done.

What everyone here knew they'd done.

Harvey's information would have to wait. Drawn to her like wind to the willows, TJ rose. She entered the dining room, gut-wrenchingly beautiful in a ruffled summer dress the color of buttercups. In her haste, she hadn't pulled up her hair, and the thick tresses flowed over her shoulders like cinnamon-shaded satin.

All that beautiful hair hanging loose gave her a slumberous look. Reminded him of how her mane had trailed over his pillow, along his arms, wound around his fist…

Their glances met for one soul-stirring second, but it was enough for him to see how much being here cost her. What she'd sacrificed by giving herself to him, forsaking Kullen as the man she claimed to love. That she believed her parents and Woollie and soon most everyone else would disdain her for betraying him.

TJ ached to reassure her he'd do what he could to save her from disgrace. Harvey's news could likely change her perspective on matters, but too soon, their glance ended. She flashed a bright smile and shifted her attention to her parents.

"Mother! Penn! I didn't expect you home so early." Striding past TJ, she embraced Carina, turned and planted a kiss on her stepfather's cheek. "Is everything all right?"

"We took the first train home as soon as we heard about what happened at Preston Farm," Carina said and dragged a quick maternal inspection over her daughter.

"Woollie told me he wired you." Callie Mae frowned at her ranch foreman. "I scolded him for it, too. I'm sure he scared you both to death. As you can see, I'm fine."

"He didn't know you were, and neither did we, until much later," Penn said. "Any parent who finds out someone put a gun to their daughter's head is entitled to get spooked."

Faces swiveled toward TJ, and he heaved a breath of regret. His methods that day were sure to haunt him for a good long while.

"It seemed the right thing to do at the time," he

admitted. "But I was all blow. I never would've pulled the trigger. I swear."

"I should hope not," Callie Mae said in quick retort. She moved toward the remaining empty chair next to TJ, but seeing the government agent, she halted in surprise. "Harvey!"

He stood, reached across the table and took her hand with a warm smile. "Good morning, Callie Mae. Yes, my arrival is most unexpected for everyone. I'm glad you're here."

"Forgive me for not noticing you sooner," she said.

TJ pulled out the chair and met her questioning glance. She eased into her seat, smoothing her skirt around her.

"Harvey has some news for us," TJ said.

"I suspected as much." Her attention slid warily back to the agent, seating himself once again.

TJ filled her cup with steaming coffee. Flapjacks smothered in strawberry jam had long been her favorite, and he slid both toward her and sat.

She unfolded a napkin over her lap; under the drape of the tablecloth, she patted his thigh in quiet thanks.

The simple gesture warmed him. It felt right to be sitting next to her like this. As if he was truly a part of her family. Sharing her life. Her troubles. Or something as ordinary as breakfast in the morning.

But Carina leaned forward and scattered his thoughts.

"We're all together now, Harvey," she said in her commanding she-boss voice. "Start from the beginning."

* * *

After he finished, thick silence hung over the table.

Callie Mae couldn't move, let alone think. She couldn't much feel, either, except excruciating hurt from what Kullen had done. The scheme he had made.

He'd duped them all. But she, of everyone, should have known.

Harvey's investigation uncovered that Kullen's real name was Brockway. Not Brosius. That his father had been a partner in the illicit counterfeit ring with her own father all those years ago. That Emmett Ralston was his cousin—and that the two of them were likely hell-bent on revenge against Penn by using Callie Mae.

And TJ.

Oh, he'd been an easy mark for Kullen. By protecting Maggie, TJ fell into Kullen's net like an apple from a tree.

TJ admitted, then, what he'd done for his mother. And why. The time was right, with all of them gathered at the table, to unlock the secret he held tight inside him. To at last reveal how his mother tried to save Danny from the stranger determined to kidnap him.

Callie Mae's parents succumbed to emotion they didn't often show, a draining mix of heartbreak and gratitude and regret. The tearful knowledge of how, in spite of the risks TJ's mother had taken, their beloved son still paid the highest price of all.

His life.

An innocent child.

Callie Mae could barely fathom how Kullen had been lying to her from the first day she met him. Had he ever loved her? Even for a moment?

He'd lied to Grandmother, too, who trusted him implicitly with her private financial affairs. He'd tricked her with a law degree which was nothing more than a sham on paper to smooth-talk his way into her money and her life.

Lies, lies, lies.

The hurt burned deeper inside Callie Mae. Could she have been more gullible? More stupid?

Finally, Harvey gathered up his reports with a heavy sigh. "As difficult as this has been, we mustn't forget Kullen and Emmett are still out there somewhere. We have to assume Kullen may try to contact Callie Mae."

"I'll see him dead first," Penn snarled.

"He's spent most of his life planning revenge against you, and he'll not walk away easily," Harvey warned.

"Then we'll make sure he doesn't walk away at all." TJ's expression was as cold, as hard, as Penn's.

Hearing their talk of vengeance, something inside Callie Mae snapped. She stood abruptly, teetering her chair back on its hind legs. "That's enough. Hasn't there been enough killing already?"

"You can't make what happened go away without a fight." But TJ reached for her to soften the harshness of his words.

She evaded him and strode toward the stairs. Not even his arms could soothe the turmoil inside her, this letting go of the man she thought she loved while knowing she had to accept he *couldn't* have loved her. Not for a single moment.

"Callie Mae, wait!"

At her mother's firm voice, she stiffly obeyed, but she refused to turn around and see the pity on everyone's faces.

"You know what must be done, Penn," Carina said firmly. "Take the others and go."

"Stay in the house, Carina. Both of you." Penn issued the order. Chairs scraped the floor.

"Go with them, TJ," Carina said.

Callie Mae didn't have to turn around to sense TJ's hesitation. She could feel his reluctance to leave as strongly as if he'd spoken it.

"I'll talk to you soon, Callie Mae," TJ said roughly. "Y'hear?"

She didn't respond. She was afraid to. The threat of tears was too strong...

"Go, TJ," her mother said, more gently this time. "She'll be fine."

After a moment, boots strode across the floor, the back door slammed, and the room fell quiet.

Her mother's tread drew nearer. Halted, right behind her. "No matter what happens, Callie Mae, there's one thing you mustn't forget."

Callie Mae finally turned. She'd heard it often enough throughout her life to know what her mother meant. "I'm a Lockett."

"Isn't that worth fighting for?"

"Of course it is." Suddenly, each of her failures darted

through her mind like stinging bees. Her disappointing meeting with the entrepreneurs. Tres Pinos Valley. Kullen. "But I'm a poor excuse for a Lockett, aren't I?"

Her mother cocked her head in puzzlement. "Why would you say that?"

"I made a terrible mistake in my choice of husband, and that's just for starters."

"Callie Mae." Her mouth curved. "Have you forgotten I thought your father would make a fine husband, too? And look where *that* got me." Reaching out, she caressed Callie Mae's cheek. "But he gave me you. My greatest treasure. And I have Penn now, so Rogan doesn't matter anymore, does he?"

Callie Mae allowed her mother's wisdom to wrap around her. "No."

"Some day, Kullen won't matter, either. In fact, I'd warrant he no longer does."

She heaved a bemused sigh. "No."

"TJ bedded you, didn't he?" Carina asked.

Callie Mae kicked up her chin. "Yes."

"If you truly loved Kullen, you never would've given TJ the privilege."

"Of course not."

"We can't let Kullen win." The avowal darkened Carina's features. "He took Danny away from us. I'll never forgive him for that. Penn and I have to make very sure Kullen and Emmett won't take the next child from us, either."

The next child?

Callie Mae's mind played with the words.

"I'm going to have another baby, sweet. In the spring." Oddly, Carina hesitated and rested a hand on her belly. "Well, two, actually."

Callie Mae blinked. "Twins?"

Eyes brightening, Carina's fingers flew to her lips; she nodded vigorously.

Callie Mae shrieked. Her arms opened, and her mother fell into them, both of them laughing and crying, and blissfully unaware...that the third step had creaked.

Chapter Eighteen

"**S**hut off the spigot to your water works, girlies, and turn around. Real easylike."

Callie Mae spun out of her mother's embrace with a gasp. Recognition of the dark, bearded face hit hard. "Oh, my God!"

Carina stepped around her. She appeared fearless standing on the wrong end of a Smith & Wesson revolver. "Get out of my house, damn you."

"Mother. It's—"

"Emmett Ralston. I know."

Another time, Callie Mae might have marveled at her mother's intuitiveness. Her calm in a bad situation. But with Callie Mae's nerves tangled like rattlesnakes, she could only comprehend that they were alone. Unarmed. And if Emmett was here, Kullen had to be close by.

"I don't have a lot of time, so I'm only goin' to say this once." Emmett took a step inside the dining room, then another. Impatience shimmered off him, like heat off a hot skillet. "Miss Lockett, you're comin' with me. Your old lady here, she can either let you go, or I'll have to smoke her up. Don't matter to me either way."

"She's not going anywhere with you," Carina spat.

His lip curled. "You're not givin' the orders around here."

"The hell I'm not." Like a proud and powerful lioness protecting her cub, she grasped Callie Mae's elbow and yanked her behind her. Her stance left no question she was ready to fight for what was hers. "Get out and leave us alone."

"Haven't you done enough already, Emmett?" Callie Mae demanded, stubbornly whipping back up to her mother's side. "Do you really think we'll let you go on hurting us?"

"Shut up!" Emmett snarled.

"We can handle him, don't you think, Mother?" she asked, watching him close. "Two against one."

"You forget who's got the shootin' iron around here?" Emmett demanded.

The man looked like a volcano ready to explode, but his stature leaned toward the small side. Her plan would be risky, but if they moved fast, combined their strengths—

"Now!" Callie Mae yelled.

Carina leapt forward and threw herself against Emmett's right arm to knock loose the weapon he wielded—but he was a split-second faster and lifted his arm before she could. With a speed neither of them predicted, he hurled his fist downward and, with the butt of his revolver, coldcocked her against the side of the head; then, he twisted and shoved Callie Mae away. She hit the wall with a force that rattled every bone in her body.

Carina cried out from his blow and hurtled backward against the table. Dishes clattered to the floor. A chair toppled. She dropped with a moan, landed in a crumpled heap and fell silent.

"Mama!" Callie Mae screamed and knelt beside her.

"I ain't never shot a woman before, but she'll be the first. I swear!" Emmett yelled, his pistol unsteady but dead-aimed at Carina's heart.

Blood oozed from an ugly gash on her head, but she was still breathing. She'd survive.

This violence against her and the tiny innocent lives inside her womb, the guilt and treachery which bombarded the Lockett legacy—Callie Mae had had enough.

Resolve pushed back fear and cleared her mind. Infused her with a boldness yet to be tested.

Until now.

She stood. Faced Emmett. Her fists doubled to contain the hatred seething through her veins. "It's me he wants. If you hurt my mother again, I swear I'll kill you."

Emmett slowly lowered the revolver. "Yeah, he wants you all right. Damned if you're worth the trouble."

Twelve long months of lies and deception. Of grief and pain and shaken hope. Callie Mae was determined to end all of it.

"Take me to him," she snapped.

Emmett's eye narrowed, as if suspicious she'd leave

Carina behind so easily. "No tricks, or I'll be the one doin' the killing. You got that?"

"Where is he?"

"He's around."

Of course he was. With his lameness, he'd use Emmett for his dirty work.

Most likely, he was on the ranch somewhere close, hiding in shadows like a coward. Places no one would think to search.

Her resolve building, she headed toward the front door, but a rough hand tangled in her hair and stopped her with a jerk. Razor-sharp tingles shot through her scalp.

"Not so fast, girlie. You think I'm stupid?" Emmett snarled in her ear. He pushed the nose of his weapon into her spine. "This place is crawlin' with cowboys. We're goin' out the back way." He yanked her in front of him, keeping her head tilted at an awkward angle, and pushed her toward the door.

Callie Mae managed to steal a sidelong glance at her mother, still unmoving, still breathing. Her heart ached from leaving her.

But she was powerless to do anything else. She would avenge Danny and make Kullen pay for what he'd done.

Or die trying.

"Did you hear that?" TJ angled his head and waited for the sound to repeat.

"Hear what?" Penn cupped his hand around the match flame, lit his cigarette, then shook the flame out.

"Not sure."

"I didn't hear anything, either." Woollie took a drag off his own stogie, but he ran a searching glance around the front yard.

"What did it sound like?" Harvey asked.

TJ didn't respond. He couldn't put his finger on it. A vague noise. From the direction of the house.

He listened again. Hard. He turned, studied the lace curtains hanging from the tall dining room window. No movement showed through. His gaze slid to the front door. Nothing unusual there, either.

But he'd heard something. What kind of noise would Callie Mae and her mother make while eating breakfast—loud enough to be heard from the outside?

Like a noxious weed, alarm took root and spread. Instinct told him a noise like that wouldn't have happened unless there was trouble. Might be he was overreacting, but already his feet had started moving, and he broke into a sprint toward the house. Took the porch stairs two at a time. Footfalls behind revealed the others picked up on his worry and ran with him.

TJ shoved open the door. "Callie Mae!"

Even before he entered the dining room, he could see the broken dishes scattered over the carpet. Icy fingers of dread clawed through his chest.

"Carina!" Penn choked an oath and hurled the fallen chair aside to get to her. Dropping to a knee, he gently slid an arm beneath her shoulders; she grimaced and moaned, and he kissed her forehead. "Carina, honey."

"Is she all right?" TJ asked roughly, kneeling, too.

"I think so." Penn smoothed away her hair, examined the cut on her head. And swore again.

"Callie Mae's gone." TJ stood, the dread slamming through him. "Damn it, he took her."

"Emmett?" Harvey asked.

"It had to be." Kullen couldn't have done it himself—not with his bum leg.

Penn's grim gaze shot to TJ's. "The rifles are in the office."

He didn't have to say more, but TJ accepted the reins of command. He turned and headed toward the room where he'd sat in the deep, over-stuffed leather chairs more times than he could remember, discussing C Bar C matters, smoking cigars, drinking whiskey. A lifetime ago.

Mounted longhorns worn by Happy Sam, one of the best steers ever to lead a C Bar C herd on the trail north, hung on the wall above the desk. In the adjoining corner, the mahogany gun cabinet took prominence. TJ opened the glass door and removed a pair of Winchester rifles, one in each hand. He tossed the first to Woollie.

"I'll come along, if you'll have me," Harvey offered. The words were no sooner spoken when he had to reach to catch the second.

Boxes of cartridges followed.

"May as well take all them shootin' sticks," Woollie said, loading fast. "We'll have to bring the whole damn outfit with us to find her."

They emptied the cabinet, and with Penn to see to

Carina, they left. Outside, on their way to the corral for horses, Jesse Keller, carrying a pitchfork, rounded the corner of the barn.

Seeing their artillery, he halted. "What the hell's going on?"

"We got trouble. Mount up," TJ ordered.

Without question, the cowboy followed. Along the way, TJ added Orlin Fahey and Billy Aspen to the group. His terse explanation of what happened had them all saddling mounts with grim expressions on their faces.

TJ swung onto his horse and speared a sharp glance at Jesse. "How the hell did Emmett get into the house anyway?"

"Damned if I know." He shoved his rifle into the scabbard. "Maybe the same way you did."

The possibility stunned him.

Through Callie Mae's window?

TJ urged his horse toward the door, dipped his head beneath the frame and once out, lifted his glance to the old oak tree growing high alongside the house. Jesse rode up next to him.

"Who was standing guard this morning?" TJ vowed vengeance on the man who let trouble in.

"Ronnie. He took the shift after mine." Jesse shot a glance toward the tree. "Come to think of it, I haven't seen him for a spell."

TJ's jaw went tight. Wasn't like the cowboy not to do what he could to protect Callie Mae. Ronnie's allegiance to Penn and Carina had never been questioned.

"TJ, look." Woollie pointed toward shrubbery growing along the foundation.

His attention latched on to a Stetson first, lying on its side in the grass, but then shifted toward movement— coming out from beneath the bushes. A man bound and gagged, awkwardly rolling toward them, slow but sure, and the mystery of Ronnie's disappearance solved itself.

They rode over to him; TJ dismounted and whipped out his knife to cut the man's own bandanna off his face and the short length of rope binding his wrists and ankles.

"Did you get a look at him?" TJ demanded, helping Ronnie to a sitting position.

Ronnie winced and probed the back of his head. "Just that he had a beard. He clunked me good and I dropped like a rock."

"Emmett." TJ gritted out the word.

"Sounds like it." Woollie nodded.

Ronnie cursed in disgust, whether at himself for being caught unawares or for what Emmett had done to him. "Son of a gun hid me in the bushes while he snuck into the house, but when I came to, I could see him leavin' the back way with Callie Mae. He was hanging on to her by her hair."

TJ drew in a slow breath. If Emmett hurt her, if he drew a single drop of her blood...

"Any idea where they went?" Jesse asked.

"Not for sure. I was plenty worried he'd remember he left me in them bushes, so I laid real still and listened real hard. I heard him say 'valley,' though, plain as paint."

Woollie connected his gaze with TJ's. "Only one valley close by."

"Tres Pinos." TJ's chin jutted in agreement.

The prettiest piece of land on the entire C Bar C.

Seemed fitting Kullen would wait for her there. He'd know Callie Mae had always wanted to live on those acres with her husband some day.

"Remember what I said, TJ," Harvey said quietly.

We have to assume Kullen will want to resume his relationship with Callie Mae in some way. In his twisted mind, he won't see marriage to her as being implausible.

TJ remembered, all right.

He stood. Adrenaline simmered in his blood. "You up to riding with us, Ronnie? We could use your help in getting Callie Mae back."

"Hell, yes, I'm up to it." The cowboy heaved himself to his feet and threw his glance over toward the bushes. "Just let me get my hat first."

But TJ had already mounted and was riding hard toward Tres Pinos Valley.

Chapter Nineteen

"Pull up. There's something I need to say to you before we go down there."

Emmett's order left Callie Mae defiant. He hadn't spoken a word to her during the ride out to Tres Pinos. Why did he have to talk now?

Her impatience to get to Kullen increased tenfold now that she could see him only a short distance away, sitting beneath a cottonwood tree, with his injured leg stretched out before him. His head rested against the tree trunk, as if he'd fallen asleep waiting for them.

"What makes you think I'd want to listen?" She dragged her attention back to Emmett.

"Cut the sass, girlie," he snapped, jabbing the Smith & Wesson at her. "I can still shoot you dead any time I want, you know."

He wouldn't shoot her, though. Callie Mae had grown confident he wouldn't. He'd gone through too much risk and danger to bring her out here.

"Now listen up," Emmett said. "He ain't himself, just so you know. His leg's botherin' him real bad, and the morphine's turned his brain to cotton. He's not thinking right."

"You should never have taken him out of the hospital," she said.

"Yeah, well, wouldn't have been long and the sheriff would've come nosin' around."

"You're a fool if you think he won't still."

"We'll be long gone before it happens." He bored a hard look at her. "If I have my way."

"Oh?" Her brow arched in disdain. "And just what might that be?"

"I'm willin' to cut you a deal."

Callie Mae hid her surprise. Emmett Ralston knew the cards were stacked against him. Kullen's injury was a detriment, a major blow to their scheme. If the cousins intended to stick together, Kullen would only slow them down…

Emmett had to know, too, time was running out. Back at the ranch, her mother would've been discovered by now. A posse of C Bar C vigilantes would've quickly formed and would be riding out even now.

"I've got a strong hankerin' to get to Mexico, Miss Lockett," Emmett said, dredging up the more respectful use of her name in his appeal. "I'm willing to take Kullen with me and make sure he never bothers you again."

She didn't have an iota of an idea how he would

manage such a thing. Did he really presume he could control a money-hungry, vengeful man like Kullen? Even injured?

"And my end of the bargain?" she asked coolly.

"Tell him he ain't got a chance in hell of marryin' you anymore." Emmett regarded her. "You know you ain't going to, besides."

It shouldn't have hurt to hear him say the words, but it did. Callie Mae had had high hopes of a lifetime of happiness with Kullen. The perfect marriage to carry on her legacy.

Yet of everyone, TJ had been the one to rock her convictions first. He'd shown her what true love was like. What love should always be. Kisses that could melt her strongest defenses, weaken her knees, fire her blood.

A love that had nothing to do with money or prestige. Conspiracy or revenge. TJ expected nothing from her in return, except, she suspected, a fragile hope that she might love him back.

But TJ wasn't here, she reminded herself firmly, and she refused to be told by a lowlife like Emmett Ralston what she should and shouldn't do.

"My relationship with Kullen is my own business," she said. "Let's get this over with."

Without waiting to see if he followed, she nudged her horse into a brisk lope toward that cottonwood tree. The long, rich grass cushioned the sound of their hooves, but not so much that Kullen shouldn't have heard their approach.

"We're back, Kullen," Emmett said in a loud voice as they pulled up. "I've got her with me."

Still, Kullen didn't rouse, and Callie Mae feared he was dead. She dismounted, noting how he still wore the expensive suit he'd donned for their meeting with the entrepreneurs in Amarillo. The fabric was dirty, one pant leg torn and bloodstained. A scruffy beard roughened his cheeks; his hair was unkempt and in need of washing. His fingers loosely gripped a whiskey bottle, and beside him in the grass, a pile of morphine vials and a syringe.

Kullen Brockway, alias Kullen Brosius, had never fallen so low.

Emmett strode over and briskly nudged his shoulder. "Wake up, Kullen."

His head lolled, then; his eyes opened. Glazed and feverish, those eyes struggled to focus. Seeing her, he grinned. Like a drunk.

"Callie, honey."

Disgust rolled through her in waves. She set her hands on her hips and glared daggers at him. "I'm not your honey, Kullen. Damn you."

"You mad at me?" He struggled to get up, swayed and would've fallen right over if Emmett hadn't been there to keep him from it. Between the two of them, however, they managed to get the job done. Kullen stood on his good leg, and braced himself on the trunk of the cottonwood.

"I'll never forgive you for what you've done to me and my family," she said.

Red-rimmed eyes darted to Emmett. "She talkin' about the boy?"

"Yes, she's talkin' about the boy!" Emmett snapped. "She ain't goin' to marry you, either, so the jig is up. Tell her how sorry you are, so we can hightail it to Mexico."

"Mexico?" Frowning, Kullen shook his head. "Don't want to go to Mexico."

Emmett fairly quaked with desperation. "We're *goin',* like we agreed."

Kullen straightened, but his expression darkened. "Goin' to live on the C Bar C. With Callie."

"You're not going to live on the C Bar C, damn it!"

"That's enough, Emmett!" Callie Mae snapped the command. "His mind is as befuddled as a child's. He's incapable of understanding you or the consequences of what you've done together." She turned to Kullen. "You're very sick, Kullen. You need to go back to the hospital."

"He's not going to the hospital."

Her glance whipped back to Emmett. "He'll die if he doesn't."

Emmett broke into agitated pacing, then halted and shot a quick look over his shoulder. As if he feared the whole C Bar C outfit might appear at any moment.

Callie Mae tasted his indecision. The battle he warred inside. "He'll never make it to Mexico, Emmett. You know that, don't you? In fact, neither of you will. So why don't you give yourself up?"

"Like hell." He swiped a hand across his mouth.

"Cooperate with the law. Maybe you'll get less jail time."

Abruptly, he stomped toward Kullen and yanked the whiskey bottle of his grasp.

"Hey!" Kullen snarled.

"Shut up!" After a couple of bracing swigs, Emmett recapped the bottle and tossed it to the ground. He blew a breath against the whiskey's burn and leveled his cousin with a spearing glance. "All right, you heard her. You're not goin' to make the trip to Mexico, so I'm headin' there without you."

"They'll find you," Callie Mae said, her heart beginning a slow pound from the knowledge that he very likely wouldn't just leave her with Kullen, both of them witnesses to his escape.

"You can't pin nothin' on me," he said.

She thought of Harvey Whelan, the detailed reports he'd made. "You'll have a price on your head. My family will put up a large reward for your arrest."

His lip curled. He cocked his Smith & Wesson. Pointed it at her, then at Kullen. And back at her again.

"Emmett, shut her up." Kullen straightened from the tree. The glaze in his eyes cleared; contempt snarled his voice, his words no longer slurred. "Y'hear me? Just knock the bitch off her high-and-mighty Lockett pedestal—"

Suddenly, he halted.

His expression turned to surprise.

And the Smith & Wesson fired.

* * *

The gunshot echoed throughout the valley, and TJ forgot to breathe.

Sweet Mother, don't let it be Callie Mae.

Woollie pointed. "Came from over there."

TJ's muscles coiled. He forced himself to think. To distance himself from the possibility Callie Mae had been killed. He had to plan. To be ready for anything when they rode into the belly of Tres Pinos Valley.

"Spread out in a circle and lay low," he ordered. "I'm going down alone. No one shoots until I give the word. And if I don't…Woollie, you're in charge."

He faced the possibility he could be killed, too. Lush, rolling hills made Tres Pinos a choice piece of rangeland, but there wasn't much out there to conceal their approach.

"We can take 'em," Woollie said. "We outnumber 'em more than three to one."

TJ refused to budge. "We don't know who's down there yet. If Callie Mae is still alive, and everyone gets trigger-happy—"

He didn't finish the sentence.

The foreman nodded. "All right. I'll cover you."

After the others rode off, TJ crested a low-rise hill and spotted yellow. He kept his horse walking while his gaze riveted to the color, his worry building that the yellow wasn't moving, that it lay too close to the ground near a cottonwood tree.

He prayed for her to move. And then, she did. To bring herself to a standing position.

TJ eased out the breath he'd been holding. Only at that moment did he see the man in the grass, the one she'd been leaning over. Wasn't long and he was close enough to tell it was Kullen Brockway.

Dead?

Almost more than he could hope for, but TJ didn't let himself become distracted by the possibility. Emmett kept his revolver pointed at Callie Mae, and that had TJ sizing up the situation in a hurry.

"Have a little tiff with your cousin, Emmett?" TJ called out. He moseyed his horse closer, giving himself the appearance of a nonchalance he was far from feeling.

Hearing him, Callie Mae whirled, but Emmett was faster, hooking his arm around her neck and shoving the nose of his pistol against her temple. Though she sank her teeth into her lower lip, she didn't cry out.

"Don't come any closer, Grier!" Emmett yelled. "I'll shoot her!"

"Easy, Emmett." TJ reined in, lifted his hands. "I'm not carrying, so you can just let her go. I'm not going to shoot you."

"You must be crazy to think I'm that stupid."

"I don't think you're stupid, Emmett." Keeping his hands up, he swung his leg over the horse's neck and slid to the ground. Thinking of his rifle tucked in its scabbard, he dared to take a step away from being armed. Two. Three. Closer to Callie Mae. "And I'm not crazy."

"Back off, y'hear me?"

Heart pounding, TJ halted.

"You alone?" Emmett's eyes darted around the valley; sweat beaded his forehead.

"Maybe," TJ said. "Maybe not."

The man snarled and shifted his stance, his nervousness growing more obvious. "I'm taking her with me, you know."

"Yeah?"

"You can't stop me."

"Don't think so?"

"I'll kill her if you try."

"It was you in the horse barn the night Danny died, wasn't it, Emmett?"

The abrupt change of topic appeared to startle him. "Hell, no, it wasn't me."

"Maggie hit you on the side of the head with her whiskey bottle. She gave you a scar, didn't she? That's why you grew a beard, to hide it. And she never recognized you."

"You can't prove nothin'. She doesn't know who she hit. I heard her talkin' about it, up at the Palo Duro. She doesn't know."

TJ's pulse lurched. *That* he hadn't expected, Emmett having been in their camp.

Damn.

But it didn't matter. Not anymore.

"Bet you didn't know my mother was left-handed." TJ continued his assault, his need to convince Emmett he was out of possibilities. "Wouldn't take much for Sheriff Dunbar to have her play out what happened for him. And I'd bet my favorite horse the scar you're wearing is on your right cheek. Because that's how she'd swing. Toward your right."

Emmett swore. He tightened his grasp around Callie Mae's neck; her breathing roughened.

TJ met her gaze and loved her for her courage. She had to be terrified. As terrified as he was. He willed her silent strength, enough for the both of them.

"Let's go, girlie. Toward the horses. C'mon." Emmett pushed her forward, and she stumbled. TJ tensed. She could fall, the Smith & Wesson could go off…

"You're surrounded," TJ snapped. "Right now, you've got six rifles trained on you."

"Six!" Emmett jerked in alarm.

"Don't believe me?"

The lowlife didn't answer. But he swallowed hard. And he didn't move.

"Woollie! Stand up!" TJ called. The foreman, lying like a sniper in the tall grass, stood, the butt of his rifle pressed to his shoulder. "Jesse!" The cowboy did the same. So did Harvey, Ronnie, Orlin, and Billy. TJ never took his eyes off Emmett. "Six rifles."

"They'll kill you, Emmett," Callie Mae said then. "Let me go, and give yourself up." She held herself stiffly against him. "It's the only way you'll get out of here alive."

"Shut up. Let's go."

"Emmett." Her voice carried threads of frustration. "We know everything. You can't deny your guilt any more."

He half-dragged her with him to their mounts, but

suddenly her foot shot out, and he tripped right over it; crying out, she twisted and rammed her fists into his chest. He grunted and grappled for balance.

TJ made his move, then, with a flying leap to tackle her to the ground, frantically shimmying over her body as a shield.

Just as six shots fired, one after the other.

And then…haunting silence.

"Won't you come in, TJ?" Callie Mae asked quietly. "My parents will want to know every detail."

He tilted his head back and studied the house. Wouldn't take much to climb the stairs and walk in, then tell Penn and Carina everything that happened in Tres Pinos Valley.

Yeah, they'd both want to know how their son's death had finally been avenged.

Trouble was, TJ wouldn't want to walk out again. He'd want to stay in that house. For the rest of his life. With Callie Mae.

But he couldn't.

The ride back to the C Bar C had been somber, to say the least. Woollie and a couple of the others had kept on going, taking the two bodies into Amarillo for burying.

TJ had taken Callie Mae home. And it was going to be hard as hell to leave her there.

"Thanks, but I think I'll head on back to Boomer's," he said. "Maggie will worry over where I've been." He managed a smile.

She hesitated, as if she regretted his answer. "Of course."

But she didn't go in just yet. Was it hard for her to see him leave? Is that why her eyes were all shimmery?

"Tres Pinos Valley is yours," she said. "You didn't know that, did you?"

"No." But he recalled her mentioning it that day she rode out to Preston Farm with Kullen. Before hell had broken loose.

Her mouth softened. "A gift from my mother to her favorite cowboy."

He'd have to think on that. The way he was feeling, after all they'd been through, he was more of an outsider than anyone's favorite.

"Guess I'll wait to see if she still wants me to have it."

It would likely be a while before she could forget his mother had been responsible for taking Danny from her, even if Maggie's intentions were the best they could be at the time.

It'd take Callie Mae a good long while to feel deserving, too. Of a husband. She'd need time to grieve for all she'd lost. Kullen hadn't always been a lowlife, at least not to her.

TJ was responsible for some of her confusion, kissing her, bedding her like he did, but he preferred to think that might help ease some of the hurt.

Even so, his chest ached for what she had ahead of her. Might be she'd swear off all men, just to protect herself.

And wouldn't that be just his luck?

He lifted a foot into the stirrup, settled himself into the saddle. Thought of all that lay ahead for him, too. Shining up the tarnish of his reputation.

He had plenty to prove to the world. To Callie Mae. Her parents. He needed them to be reminded of the man he'd always been, deep inside.

Time. They both needed it.

"Goodbye, Callie Mae."

"TJ, I—" She halted. Bit her lip. "Never mind."

He nudged his horse forward, and as he rode down the lane toward Boomer's, he could feel her watching him go.

Epilogue

Callie Mae shaded her eyes against the late-morning sun and riveted a fascinated gaze to the gaily striped hot-air balloon slowly ascending into the sky.

"You couldn't pay me enough to climb into one of those contraptions." Her mother gently rocked the extra-wide woven-reed carriage. Inside, Callie Mae's baby brothers slept soundly, oblivious to the sporting crowds that packed the Panhandle Exposition. "They make my stomach flutter just looking at them."

"Mmm. But think of the adventure, Mother."

"I can only think of falling out."

Callie Mae laughed softly. "Yes, I suppose I'd think of that, too."

Even so, the excitement of her first hot-air balloon ride was something she intended to experience at some point in her future.

But not today. There were too many other things to see and do.

Like her first formal stakes horse race.

Reconsidering her decision to allow the entrepreneurs to build their exposition on leased C Bar C land not far from Tres Pinos Valley had never felt more right. She had Danny to thank for that. The truth in his death. Knowing he hadn't really died as a result of the forbidden racing, and the drinking and wagering that encompassed it, well, her perspective took on a big change.

Besides, all the excitement in the air was catching.

The scent of fresh lumber and new paint still hovered over the grandstands, an elegant roofed structure of which every row was filled. Those that couldn't find seats milled on the ground, talking and laughing. Each woman came dressed in her finest gown, each man in his best Sunday suit.

Others gathered along the track, surrounded on both sides by a white wooden fence. Near the finish line, bookmakers worked the betting ring, posting their calculated odds on elevated blackboards. Harlots mingled with the upright; penne-ante gamblers with high-stakes operators.

"They're getting ready to race." Carina pointed to the starting line.

Callie Mae shifted her scrutiny to the horses, brought out from the paddocks by their trainers and led to their places. Anticipation quickened her pulse. Seven beautiful thoroughbreds, ridden by jockeys in colorful silks.

Yet she lifted her binoculars and focused the lenses over only one horse. Blue Whistler. Gleaming black beneath the sun, thickly muscled and long-legged, Lord, he was something to behold.

"Amazing how he's won every race he's ever run, isn't it?" Carina murmured, studying him, too.

Callie Mae didn't need to consult her racing bill to know it was true. Newspapers continually carried enthusiastic headlines proclaiming the thoroughbred's prowess on the dirt track.

"Seems he got everything he wanted with that horse," her mother mused.

Callie Mae refused to look at her. "Who?"

"You know very well who."

She lowered the glasses. "I suppose you mean TJ."

Just saying his name out loud stirred the blood in her veins. After that fateful day when he'd ridden away from the C Bar C, Callie Mae had avoided speaking about him unnecessarily.

It was easier that way.

Eventually, her parents quit talking about him at all, at least not in her presence, and that suited her fine.

But oh, she still missed him. So much, it hurt. How many nights had she lain awake, hoping to hear her window open, wishing he'd crawl right through and into her bed?

Too many, for sure.

Unfortunately, the man hadn't bothered to step foot on C Bar C soil in the months since, so why should she waste her breath on him?

"You'll feel better if you swallow some of that pride, you know," Carina said in that shrewd way of hers.

"Hush, Mother." Callie Mae refused to discuss TJ further. Matters between them wouldn't change, so what was the use? "The starter is raising his pistol."

Again, she fastened the glasses over Blue Whistler. At the sharp report, the horses bolted forward. Their hooves pounded over the track, fast, faster. The cheers of the crowd nearly drowned out the thundering sound, and oh, the excitement of watching them!

Her lenses followed Blue around the track, and she forgot to breathe. He pulled forward with an ease that astounded her, astounded everyone, increasing his lead with every second, until a length and a half separated him from the horse behind.

And before she knew it, the race was over.

Blue Whistler had won again.

The crowd roared its excitement. Callie Mae cheered, too. Even her mother got caught up in the commotion—until the deafening noise awakened the babies.

No amount of soothing could quiet their squalls, and Carina was compelled to search for someplace private to feed them. Knowing her mother would need help, Callie Mae accompanied her in a roundabout route past the grandstands, until oddly, Carina halted.

"Why, there's the winner's circle," she said.

Captivated by the magnificent Blue Whistler, Callie Mae halted, too. The thoroughbred was surrounded by scores of people, photographers and reporters madly jotting notations on their pads. Still in the saddle, Lodi, the jockey, mud-spattered but exultant, held a bouquet of roses. A beaming Boomer Preston kept firm hold on the bridle while his new wife, Maggie, clutched his elbow and smiled shyly for the cameras.

And in the midst of all of them…TJ.

Her breath left her in a whoosh. If she thought him blood-warming virile in Levi's and cotton shirt, he was doubly so now in a crisp black suit and pristine white shirt. His teeth gleamed from a broad smile; his skin had been darkened from the sun. He appeared completely at ease as the center of attention, answering questions smoothly, with a quick wit.

"Mr. Grier, Blue Whistler's win today has won you a purse thousands of dollars richer than formal stakes races back East. How does that make you feel, being a wealthy man?" one of the reporters called out.

"Guess I'd have to say it makes me feel proud of my horse. None of this would be happening if not for him. And—"

He spied Callie Mae, then, and the words died in his throat.

Heads turned toward her, and instant embarrassment from being caught eavesdropping swept through her. She yanked her gaze away and would've escaped with her mother…except her mother had left, pushing the carriage through the crowd at a fast pace, which made Callie Mae realize with absolute and appalling certainty that her mother had been cleverly matchmaking—

Panicked, Callie Mae turned back to TJ.

She recognized the expectant hush which had fallen over the group surrounding him. Being a Lockett, she'd experienced it often enough, and the years of bearing her name had taught her what to do.

She squelched the panic. Ignored the pounding of her heart. She squared her shoulders, strode forward and met the curious looks head on. She planted a smile on her face. She extended her hand and opened her mouth to express her congratulations to TJ—except a brash, unimpressed reporter stepped in front of her without regard to her intentions, bumped her sideways and nearly knocked her off her feet.

"Mr. Grier, tell us what other races you've assigned Blue Whistler to run," he said in a loud voice.

TJ scowled at him. "That's enough questions, gentlemen." He grasped Callie Mae's elbow. "Are you all right?"

"I think so." She righted her hat, a delicate creation of straw, ribbons and one very prominent ostrich feather.

"Come with me."

"Where are we going?" she asked, as he burrowed his way through well-wishers with a ruthless charm. "What about Blue and those people who were waiting to talk to you?"

"Boomer will take care of 'em."

He hustled her toward the Amarillo Jockey Club, and they passed Henry Sanborn along the way. Joseph Glidden and James T. Berry, too, the entrepreneurs who'd been so determined to build the exposition and its racetrack. She had no time to speak with them, not when she had to hurry to keep up with TJ's long-legged stride.

He pushed open the club doors; the scent of cigars and leather accosted her. He guided her through the dining room and down a hall, finally turning into a smoking room of sorts, elegantly done in dark wall paneling and large, overstuffed chairs.

He locked the door. And speared her with his hooded gaze.

"What took you so long, Callie Mae?" he demanded.

She blinked up at him. "What do you mean?"

"I thought you'd come to see Blue before now. Hell, after all we went through to steal him away from the mustangs, didn't you want to see him run?"

Her mind worked. "I was waiting for *you* to come back to the C Bar C, TJ. You never called on me. You never—I thought you—"

"I've been traveling. Have been for weeks." He cocked his jaw. "Guess you could say I've gotten a few things out of my system while I was gone."

Callie Mae understood. The dream he'd needed to follow.

"You've always been a fine horseman, TJ. Now you're an accomplished turfman, too. You've become respected in racing. People envy you for what you've done. Has that been enough?"

"No."

She regarded him with surprise.

"All the months I spent on the circuit convinced me it wasn't the life for me. I want a home of my own,

Callie. Not in a bunkhouse on the C Bar C. Not in a spare room at Boomer's. My own house. My own land."

"Yes." She understood that, too. Hadn't she wanted those same things? "But you can. In Tres Pinos Valley."

"Your mother offered the acres to me. And I accepted, on two conditions. The first, I would buy them from her fair and square. I didn't want those acres just because I happened to be her favorite cowboy."

TJ had amassed considerable wealth in racing Blue. Buying the land from her parents, at almost any price, would meet the condition.

"I've missed you, Callie Mae," he said suddenly. "There were times when I thought it would just about eat me alive, missing you so much."

Unexpected hope stirred inside her, like baby butterfly wings. "I've missed you, too." There. She admitted it. "I could hardly bear being away from you."

Their gazes locked, and a slow heat darkened the depths of his eyes. He hooked his arm around her waist and brought her full against him, lowered his head and took her mouth with a sudden savagery that revealed the yearnings he'd kept inside him too long. She melted. Of their own accord, her arms curled around his back, and only by feeding his hunger could she sate her own.

She had no way of knowing how long he kissed her, only that her lips turned swollen, her breathing ragged. He dragged his mouth along her jaw, pressed kisses into the curve of her neck.

"Oh, TJ, I've wanted you to hold me like this for so long," she murmured. "I've wanted to taste you, love you, like I did when you crawled in through my bedroom window."

Her lashes drifted closed; she savored all the delicious things he made her feel.

But there was more she needed to know. She drew back.

"What of the second condition?" she asked, holding her breath.

"Ah, that's the best condition of all." Despite his smile, he seemed to hesitate. "That I share the land with you. Fifty-fifty. As my wife. For the rest of our lives."

Her breath caught. Her throat closed with a surge of emotion.

"Are you asking me to marry you?" she whispered.

"I'll build you the house you've always wanted, Callie Mae. We'll fill it with our children." He kissed her again, so tenderly she nearly wept.

Happiness soared through her. Had her mother known all along?

"I love you, TJ," she breathed. "Even when I didn't know I did, I loved you."

"But I loved you even more."

Her heart swelled near to breaking. "Yes. I think you did. But only at first."

"Will you marry me, darlin'?"

"Yes. Oh, TJ."

Callie Mae sealed the vow with a plethora of kisses.

She reveled in the knowledge that he was coming back home to the C Bar C, at last, to be her very own—and very favorite—cowboy. And that he intended to stay, for the rest of their lives.

To live their very own legacy.

* * * * *

Love Inspired.
HISTORICAL

Powerful, engaging stories of romance, adventure and faith set in the past—when life was simpler and faith played a major role in everyday lives.

See below for a sneak preview of
HIGH COUNTRY BRIDE
by Jillian Hart

Love Inspired Historical—love and faith throughout the ages

Silence remained between them, and she felt the rake of his gaze, taking her in from the top of her wind-blown hair where escaped tendrils snapped in the wind to the toe of her scuffed, patched shoes. She watched him fist up his big, work-roughened hands and expected the worst.

"You never told me, Miz Nelson. Where are you going to go?" His tone was flat, his jaw tensed as if he were still fighting his temper. His blue gaze shot past her to watch the children going about their picking up.

"I don't know." Her throat went dry. Her tongue felt thick as she answered. "When I find employment, I could wire a payment to you. Rent. Y-you aren't thinking of bringing the sher-riff in?"

"You think I want *payment?*" He boomed like winter thunder. *"You think I want rent money?"*

"Frankly, I don't know what you want."

"I'll tell you what I don't want. I don't want—" His

words cannoned in the silence as he paused, and a passing pair of geese overhead honked in flat-noted tones. He grimaced, and it was impossible to know what he would say or do.

She trembled, not from fear of him, she truly didn't believe he would strike her, but from the unknown. Of being forced to take the frightening step off the only safe spot she'd known since she'd lost Pa's house.

When you were homeless, everything seemed so fragile, so easily off balance, for it was a big, unkind world for a woman alone with her children. She had no one to protect her. No one to care. The truth was, she'd never had those things in her husband. How could she expect them from any stranger? Especially this man she hardly knew, who was harsh and cold and hardhearted.

And, worse, what if he brought in the law?

"You can't keep living out of a wagon," he said, still angry, the cords still straining in his neck. "Animals have enough sense to keep their young cared for and safe."

Yes, it was as she'd thought. He intended to be as cruel about this as he could be. She spun on her heel, pulling up all her defenses, and was determined to let his upcoming hurtful words roll off her like rainwater on an oiled tarp. She grabbed the towel the children had neatly folded and tossed it into the laundry box in the back of the wagon.

"Miz Nelson. I'm talking to you."

"Yes, I know. If you expect me to stand there while you tongue lash me, you're mistaken. I have packing to get to." Her fingers were clumsy as she hefted the bucket of water she'd brought for washing—she wouldn't need that now—and heaved.

His hand clasped on the handle beside hers, and she could feel the life and power of him vibrate along the thin metal. "Give it to me."

Her fingers let go. She felt stunned as he walked away, easily carrying the bucket that had been so heavy to her, and quietly, methodically, put out the small cooking fire. He did not seem as ominous or as intimidating—somehow—as he stood in the shadows, bent to his task, although she couldn't say why that was. Perhaps it was because he wasn't acting the way she was used to men acting. She was quite used to doing all the work.

Jamie scurried over, juggling his wooden horses, to watch. Daisy hung back, eyes wide and still, taking in the mysterious goings-on.

He is different when he's near to them, she realized. He didn't seem harsh, and there was no hint of anger—or, come to think of it, any other emotion—as he shook out the empty bucket, nodded once to the children and then retraced his path to her.

"Let me guess." He dropped the bucket onto the tailgate, and his anger appeared to be back. Cords strained in his neck and jaw as he growled at her. "If you leave here, you don't know where you're going and you have no money to get there with?"

She nodded. "Yes, sir."

"Then get you and your kids into the wagon. I'll

hitch up your horses for you." His eyes were cold and yet they were not unfeeling as he fastened his gaze on hers. "I have an empty shanty out back of my house that no one's living in. You can stay there for the night."

"What?" She stumbled back, and the solid wood of the tailgate bit into the small of her back. "But—"

"There will be no argument," he bit out, interrupting her. "None at all. I buried a wife and son years ago, what was most precious to me, and to see you and them neglected like this—with no one to care—" His jaw ground again and his eyes were no longer cold.

Joanna didn't think she'd ever seen anything sadder than Aiden McKaslin as the sun went down on him.

* * * * *

Don't miss this deeply moving story,
HIGH COUNTRY BRIDE,
available July 2008
from the new Love Inspired Historical line.

Also look for SEASIDE CINDERELLA
by Anna Schmidt,
where a poor servant girl and a
wealthy merchant prince
might somehow make a life together.

HARLEQUIN®
Super Romance®

Lawyer Audrey Lincoln has sworn off
love, throwing herself into her work
instead. When she meets a much younger
cop named Ryan Mercedes, all her logic
is tossed out the window, and Ryan is
determined that he will not let the issue
of age come between them. It is not until
a tragic case involving an innocent child
threatens to tear them apart that Ryan
and Audrey must fight for a way to
finally be together....

Look for

TRUSTING RYAN

by Tara Taylor Quinn

*Available July
wherever you buy books.*

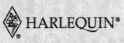

HARLEQUIN®

American ★ Romance®

MADE IN TEXAS

It's the happiest day of Hannah Callahan's life
when she brings her new daughter home to Texas.
And Joe Daugherty would make a perfect father
to complete their unconventional family. But the
world-hopping writer never stays in one place
long enough. Can Joe trust in love enough to
finally get the family he's always wanted?

LOOK FOR

Hannah's Baby

BY

CATHY GILLEN THACKER

Available July
wherever you buy books.

LOVE, HOME & HAPPINESS

REQUEST YOUR FREE BOOKS!

Harlequin® Historical
Historical Romantic Adventure!

2 FREE NOVELS PLUS 2 FREE GIFTS!

YES! Please send me 2 FREE Harlequin® Historical novels and my 2 FREE gifts (gifts are worth about $10). After receiving them, if I don't wish to receive any more books, I can return the shipping statement marked "cancel". If I don't cancel, I will receive 6 brand-new novels every month and be billed just $4.94 per book in the U.S. or $5.49 per book in Canada, plus 25¢ shipping and handling per book and applicable taxes, if any*. That's a savings of 20% off the cover price! I understand that accepting the 2 free books and gifts places me under no obligation to buy anything. I can always return a shipment and cancel at any time. Even if I never buy another book, the two free books and gifts are mine to keep forever.

246 HDN ERUM   349 HDN ERUA

Name	(PLEASE PRINT)	
Address		Apt. #
City	State/Prov.	Zip/Postal Code

Signature (if under 18, a parent or guardian must sign)

Mail to the **Harlequin Reader Service:**
IN U.S.A.: P.O. Box 1867, Buffalo, NY 14240-1867
IN CANADA: P.O. Box 609, Fort Erie, Ontario L2A 5X3

Not valid to current subscribers of Harlequin Historical books.

Want to try two free books from another line?
Call 1-800-873-8635 or visit www.morefreebooks.com.

* Terms and prices subject to change without notice. N.Y. residents add applicable sales tax. Canadian residents will be charged applicable provincial taxes and GST. Offer not valid in Quebec. This offer is limited to one order per household. All orders subject to approval. Credit or debit balances in a customer's account(s) may be offset by any other outstanding balance owed by or to the customer. Please allow 4 to 6 weeks for delivery. Offer available while quantities last.

Your Privacy: Harlequin Books is committed to protecting your privacy. Our Privacy Policy is available online at www.eHarlequin.com or upon request from the Reader Service. From time to time we make our lists of customers available to reputable third parties who may have a product or service of interest to you. If you would prefer we not share your name and address, please check here. ☐

HH08R

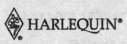

COMING NEXT MONTH FROM

HARLEQUIN®
HISTORICAL